BONEYARD BABIES

ALSO BY ALAN M. CLARK

The Paint in My Blood

Pain & Other Petty Plots to Keep You in Stitches

Siren Promised (w/ Jeremy Robert Johnson)

D.D. Murphry, Secret Policeman (w/ Elizabeth Massie)

The Christmas Thingy (w/ F. Paul Wilson)

The Halloween Mouse (w/ Richard Laymon)

The Blood of Father Time duology
    (w/ Lorelei Shannon and Stephen C. Merritt)

BONEYARD BABIES

ALAN M. CLARK

Lazy Fascist Press
Portland, OR

LAZY FASCIST PRESS
830 SW 18TH AVENUE
PORTLAND, OR 97205

WWW.LAZYFASCIST.COM

ISBN: 1-936383-21-7

Cover art copyright © 2010 by Alan M. Clark
www.alanmclark.com

Interior art copyright © 2010 by Alan M. Clark

Printed in the USA.

ACKNOWLEDGMENTS

AUTHOR'S NOTE

There are two types of stories in this collection, ones that make sense and ones that do not. I'll let the ones that do make sense speak for themselves. The ones that do not deserve a little explanation and with it a little history.

I am primarily a visual artist, but in the 1970s while living and going to school in San Francisco, I began to write as yet another means of creative expression. I smoked marijuana with my roommate and then we tried to write bizarre stories. It was fun collaborating and laughing about what we came up with. Our tendency was to try to write a solid story with a beginning, middle and end, an antagonist, a protagonist, conflict and resolution. But being high, it was difficult for me to focus on telling a character-driven story that didn't wander off and get lost in the thick forest of my imagination. I think he had the same problem. Over time we became frustrated as the unfinished, hopeless stories piled up.

The solution was to stop making sense. Being a surrealist at heart, I believe in the power of the subconscious to offer up creative solutions. I proposed to my roommate a writing game that would prevent us from concentrating on creating reasonable story elements.

The process put us in a position of having to find a story through free-association. What we ended up with definitely did not make sense in a conventional way, but it felt like a story and seemed complete. When reading it, my imagination did its best to assign meaning to the text, creating a surreal cartoon for my mind's eye.

Here are the rules of the game I call Bone-Grubber's Gamble:

1) Two writers each create ten partial sentences of bizarre content and then trade them with one another.

2) A simple open-ended premise for a story is agreed upon (My roommate and I decided the first one of these we wrote would be about TWO BEST FRIENDS WHO HATE EACH OTHER).

3) A coin is flipped to see who will go first.

4) The winning writer chooses one of his counterpart's sentences and begins the story. The sentence can be kept as-is and completed or changed in any way, or it could be just a springboard for ideas. Sentences don't have to make sense, but they should still have good structure.

When the first writer is finished, the other writer takes a turn and they alternate turns until the story finds its own end. This usually occurs within the first two pages. As the writers take turns, they keep in mind that connective tissue in the form of repeated words and concepts helps tie sentences, paragraphs and ultimately the story together and give a sense that the story is whole even if it is truly nonsensical.

Below is an example of a set of partial sentences of bizarre content that I generated this year while looking through a book on torture devices. I sent them to Eric M. Witchey to use when we wrote the story titled "Conrad's New Shoe Goo."

1) where harmless humans, roasted and boiled to little cubes

2) every apology a death penalty

3) fervent prayers became an iron gag and a drunkard of gin

4) four claws and a high-end adultery appliance

5) a heresy of corndogs and chocolate-dipped

6) hankered after the older and more popular atrocities

7) would have four testicles instead of the usual tub of lard

8) bespectacled himself by stretching out his naked erection

9) hadn't screamed puppet warnings in over a decade

10) wake unto waist rings and pyramid points

This is not about the story. After all, some of them don't make sense. It's about how nimble the imagination is, both the writer's and the reader's.

The table of contents is broken into three sections. The first, "Older, More Popular Atrocities," is made up of stories that are more traditional and are not arrived at by means of the Bone-Grubber's Gamble. The second section, "A Heresy of CornDogs," is composed of stories that were arrived at by means of the Bone-Grubber's Gamble, but developed with an eye toward making more traditional stories. The third section is pure Bone-Grubber's Gamble. Several of these stories I wrote by myself. This required me to assemble at least twenty partial sentences and to pretend to be two writers.

Alan M. Clark
Eugene, Oregon

TABLE OF CONTENTS

THE SENSE IN NONSENSE

An Introduction by Eric M. Witchey

When Alan M. Clark asked me if I'd be interested in doing a little experiment in nonsense with him, my first response was to say yes because I like Alan and we always have fun when we do something together. When he showed me what he wanted to do, I was a little dubious about the market value of the experiment. However, I decided to do it anyway. He showed me some examples of the "nonsense" stories he and others had come up with, and I was intrigued by the fact that as I read them, I could feel my brain churning away trying to create meaning from them. It reminded me of the feeling I get when I read those emails people send around that show how you can read the words even if the letters are scrambled as long as the frist and lsat lttres are the smae. That triggered a memory from long ago.

When I was in graduate school studying Theoretical Linguistics at Colorado State University, I ran across some interesting articles on how people organize and draw meaning from text. Actually creating a couple of experimental stories with Alan made me realize that we were taking advantage of the phenomena described in the articles I'd used twenty-five years ago in my thesis.

Human perception is all about pattern matching. Pretty much everybody agrees on that. One of the interesting questions is where the original patterns come from and what they are. I'm not here to get involved in answering the question of whether nature or nurture dominate human development. But I am here to shed a little light on why these odd little literary experiments work, or in some cases don't work, as entertainments for readers.

First, it's important to notice that I said, "for readers." If people haven't had exposure to a lot of stories, these experiments are much less likely to work. Why? Because according to the studies I mentioned, story structure is learned within the context of culture. That is, by the time we're six or so, assuming our parents and the world around us exposed us to many stories, we've internalized the patterns that make a story in the same way we've internalized the patterns that make a sentence. Every first grader can tell you that the sentence, "She took her ball and. . ." isn't finished. And every child of a certain age can tell if you decide to cheat by reading half a story, closing the book, and saying, "And they lived happily ever after." They can tell even if they've never heard that story before.

What Teun A. van Dijt and Walter Kintsch, the authors of the studies I used way back then, were doing was trying to figure out what those structures were. Mind you, they weren't looking at dramatic structures like we writers do. They were looking at schematic structures, the constituents that are necessary to allow a reader to comprehend a block of text and its relationship to other blocks of text. Just like the scrambled letters word recognition trick, it turns out that if all the pieces are there to make up a complete story, it doesn't matter what their order is. The reader can understand it.

So, what are the pieces?

Kintsch, who later went on to coin the term "chunking" in cognitive science, showed that a reader was constantly looking for coherent chunks to accumulate and collapse into components of a story. He described the reader's organization of micro-schematic elements into macro-schematic elements. Because of this, we are able to understand the plight of a character confronted with an obstacle because we can accumulate meaning from the sentences that appear before us, provided they give us a sense of completeness themselves.

To map this concept onto a few traditional story elements, let's look at a character in a setting with a problem:

Once upon a time, there was a little girl with golden hair who had become lost in the woods.

The little bits add up to a part of the template we recognize as a part of story. The micro elements readers glean are time, place, person, problem. As a group, the reader organizes them into a pre-known template and feels a sense of completion. If you stop reading to your child at this point, they kick you and say, "Then what happened?" The child knows that once you have character, setting, and problem, stuff has to happen.

So, here, the sentences make sense, each contributes a micro element to a larger macro element.

Time+place+character+problem = story beginning.

The rest of the story, any story, has similar characteristics. If you think about it, it makes perfect sense. Written story is, after all, an artifact of language in the same way as a word or a sentence. One of the pillars of the function of language is syntax. So, it follows that we would have a syntax of story, albeit considerably more generative and sophisticated than sentence-level syntax.

So, if we look at a block of text and are able to see patterns that remind us of the syntax of a story, our pattern matching minds will try to make that block of text into a story.

Teun A. van Dijt did a little different work with the same concepts. He took stories and broke them up into constituent parts then scrambled them. He then tested a group of people to determine how well they could reconstruct a story that had been read in a scrambled format. Of course, he also measured the results from a control group who had read the same story in its normal order.

What he found was wonderful and accounts for why stories like *The Sixth Sense* work so well when done artfully. It turned out that it didn't take any longer for a reader to recount the story in the correct order when they read a scrambled version than it did when they read an unscrambled version. In other words, not only is the reader constantly organizing, chunking the patterns in a story, they are also instantly revising all the chunks they've already accumulated. This revision strives to organize the chunks and their contents into the story patterns learned as developing children.

The consequence of these amazing tricks of the mind is that when a reader comes to the experiments in this book, they can't help but attempt to organize the material into a coherent story in spite of the fact that the text is, essentially, nonsense. As long as the text suggests to the reader's pattern matcher that it might eventually make sense, the brain has at it in an attempt to put all the pieces together until there's a happily ever after for reader and story.

While these experiments may not all deliver a sense of completion to the reader, they do engage the reader's story-finding brain. Most importantly, these stories take the reader on a ride they could never go on in any other kind of story.

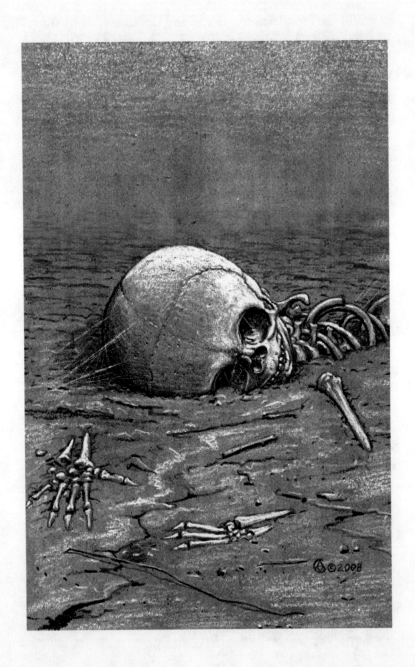

PART I

OLDER, MORE POPULAR ATROCITIES

BRITTLE STICKS AND OLD ROPE

Little Dylan died when he was five years old and was laid to rest. Although he was stuck in the withering body of a child, he had grown emotionally in the ten years he'd spent in the little graveyard. Grieving for his lost life, while it didn't make him feel whole, was enough for a long time. But lately, his grief had run out, leaving him with a hole in his heart and a purposeless existence. He might have considered passing on, but that was too frightening to think about.

The other dead who remained here, seven of them altogether, went about their business as if what they did was important, and it seemed to give them a sense of purpose.

Jewel Cornsby was using honeysuckle vine to reattached one of the baby's arm bones. She always took good care of the baby, even when it seemed a losing battle.

Miss Omer was sitting under a tree humming the same song over and over. She was senile when she died and still was.

Clay Potts, pacing dangerously close to the border of the graveyard, was ranting about visitors again. "Why don't they use the gravel drive instead of wanderin' across the field and trampling the crops?" Clay owned the surrounding farm when he was alive and was none too happy about the way it was currently run. He was a grouch.

Clay's wife, Betty, squatting at the edge of a rain puddle and molding an ear out of mud, didn't so much as look up.

"Clay, it's no longer your property or your concern."

Betty, besides being Clay's wife, was Miss Omer's half sister. Dylan thought that was an unfair way to refer to the woman. True, she had lost the left half her face in a car accident, but it wasn't actually half her whole self so she shouldn't have to be known as a "half sister," Dylan thought.

The Rampert brothers, Ned and Epply, were playing cards with dead leaves. "Goddamn ace!" Ned shouted, grabbing up a leaf and shredding it. Epply's dry laugh was more a whispered moan. The brothers were bullies who were usually up to no good.

It all seemed rather meaningless to Dylan, except maybe Jewel's concern for the baby. But what did he know? He was just a stupid kid.

Dylan was handicapped in understanding the things people did when those things were reflections of what they had done in life. The others had all had a lifetime of experiences that made their thoughts and actions complex, but his memories of life were a bit choppy and mixed up. He wasn't even sure what killed him.

"Sounds to me like it was chicken pox did you in," Betty had once said after he described what he could recall. But Dylan couldn't remember ever being around chickens except for those he and his family ate, and they didn't have beaks.

Jewel was the nicest. Dylan thought she was a prime candidate for passing on to a wonderful reward. She was a tolerant woman who never had an unkind word for anyone. She remained here for reasons unclear to Dylan. He'd overheard her ask Betty, "Do you think God punishes adulterers the same as thieves and murderers?"

Dylan wondered why she would ask that when everyone became an adult if they lived long enough. Wasn't that the way it was supposed to be? Betty's response made so little sense to him he'd forgotten it.

Dylan thought what really held Jewel back had something

to do with the baby. It was a pitiful thing. Jewel considered it female, but there was no way to really know its gender. It lolled around not ever doing much of anything but deteriorating, occasionally getting stepped on, being patched up with mud, dried grass, and gravel by the women. It had been here longer than any of the current residents, and it showed. There was little tissue left on its bones, its joints were giving way, and it was tied back together in more places than it was not.

When Dylan first arrived in the graveyard, he'd hated the baby and didn't know why. Perhaps it was because its slow movements and the long, hissing cry that emerged from its broken, toothless grin were disturbing. He knew Jewel loved it and he had been jealous of that for a while, but now, for her sake, he tried to warm to the tiny creature. Over time his feelings toward it had softened.

He recognized Jewel's efforts to take care of the baby as meaningful. It was a reflection of the kindness and concern she showed all of them. It was especially important for a helpless, permanent infant, but he could see that it also helped Jewel.

It was exactly the sort of thing he was looking for to help him fill the hole in his heart. But it was Jewel's and he needed to find his own thing. What could he do that would be that helpful, perhaps even heroic?

"Sumbitch—Lookit," Clay shouted, "here come some more of 'em."

Dylan looked up to see three visitors approaching. They moved about in fast-motion. Like nervous mice, Dylan thought.

"I'll seat them and take their orders," Miss Omer said as she lurched off in their direction. Although she was in her eighties when she died, she hadn't been here very long and so she was a lot more agile than Dylan. He rose stiffly to his feet and followed slowly.

Like moth's to a flame, the inhabitants of the graveyard were attracted to the living whenever they turned up, so fascinated by their presence and light that they tended to forget the world around them. Dylan loved to listen to the living. He knew, based on the speed these visitors were moving, their voices would be high-pitched. Like mice, he thought again. This time, it was accompanied by a memory of white mice with pink eyes he'd seen in a pet store when he was alive. It was so delightful he momentarily forgot the pain in his joints and dried tissues. Maybe, if time slowed while the visitors were here, he'd get a chance to touch their living flesh. That was the best way to soothe the pain, if only temporarily.

Everyone had gotten way ahead of him as they moved to warm their imaginations by the glow of the living. Dylan quickened his pace the best he could when it occurred to him that Dot Morrisy and Jim Thaber had gone missing, each on an occasion when everyone's attention was focused on living visitors.

Had someone forced Dot and Jim to pass on? Just yesterday Betty Potts said, "I believe there is a murderer among us."

Her husband was dismissive. "You read too many mysteries in your day, woman."

Even so, Dylan had been looking over his shoulder ever since. Not that the dead could be killed, but perhaps they could be forced to enter the surrounding fields. The graveyard was their anchor. If any of them travelled more than ten paces away from its borders they would not be seen again. They would pass on into the great unknown. Were Dot and Jim victims because they didn't stick with the others and were easy pickings while everyone was distracted?

Sometimes Dylan thought of passing on as a relief and a release from the growing pain in the drying husk of his body. All the dead experienced the pain and it grew in intensity the longer they remained. Some couldn't stand it any longer and decided to pass on, but those who'd recently disappeared were relatively fresh and had expressed no such inclination. It was frightening to think the choice might be taken away from Dylan, or from anyone for that matter.

Hey, that's it—I'll figure out who the murderer is. That would be meaningful, even heroic. This was a really great idea and he was becoming excited.

At that moment all the dead up ahead of him stop short at the same time. All, that is, but Miss Omer. Then he saw the reason—one of the visitors was carrying something with shiny metal parts. Dylan sort of recognized it, but couldn't remember what it was called. It seemed Miss Omer had forgotten or still didn't understand that iron was the one thing carried by the living that could do the dead real damage. Her memory was very bad, but her understanding of the issue was also hampered by the fact that she'd never really understood she was dead.

"Miss Omer," Jewel called out, "you stay well away from those people. They're moving awful fast and that one fellow's got an umbrella."

Miss Omer was heedless of the warning. Headless if she's not careful, Dylan thought. He knew better than to try to stop her. Oh well, they could always patch her up later. He turned his back, not wanting to watch what might happen to the old woman.

Seeing the baby where Jewel had left it, lying at the base of a tree, Dylan plopped onto the ground beside it. He was sore from all the movement and disappointed his chance to touch the living would come to nothing. It wasn't much, but it felt like a large loss in such a small world.

It put a damper on his excitement. As he returned to thinking about his idea, he realized whoever was murdering was doing it secretly and he didn't know how to penetrate secrets. How could he accomplish anything meaningful if he couldn't think these things through? Boy was he stupid.

Dylan didn't trust his own mind because his memories of what few life experiences he'd had were frequently inaccurate. This included some of his most vivid memories, like the time he and his family had been picnicking and he was looking for the butter knife to spread more jelly on his roll. When he asked his mother where it was, she'd said with a giggle, "Oh, honey, you swallowed it."

That was difficult to believe, but when his father, a doctor who Dylan trusted to tell him the truth about such things, confirmed it, saying, "Don't worry, son, it'll pass right on through," Dylan had to accept it. The big, warm smile his father had given him was one of the few things he'd thought he could count on in life.

When he'd told others here in the graveyard the story, they laughed at him, some belittling him. He was told it was impossible, his parents were only making a fool of him because he was gullible. Dylan supposed that was more possible than swallowing a butter knife, but he even had a vague memory of the cold steel sliding down his throat. Where had that come from, his imagination? Or was it real? Was the butter knife still in there cutting the hole in his heart?

He didn't really know what to believe. He felt bad. He blamed himself. Dylan was more than gullible and stupid, he was somehow broken. As a human being, he just wasn't right. All of his memories of when he was alive were suspect. As Dylan looked back along the lengthening tunnel of his memory, life—the beautiful light at the opening—was rapidly fading into the distance. He feared one day soon it might wink out, and he struggled to gain an understanding of it before that happened. He felt this understanding would give him definition and maybe fix him.

The existence of a "murderer" in their midst gave his quest for understanding all the more urgency. That he might suddenly be even further removed from life was terrifying.

The best way to learn more about his own life was to find out what life had been for the others here. Lately he'd had many questions for Jewel, Betty and Clay. He used their answers as evidence to help him confirm or deny his own memories, to sort out what was real from what was not. This was a long, slow process as he tried not to tell them what he remembered from life since he didn't want them to laugh at him. "The two women were very understanding and helpful, while Clay showed nothing but impatience. "You ask the weirdest questions, kid. What are you gonna do, write a book or something?"

"Does it hurt you to answer his questions, Clay?" Betty had asked. "You should be glad he's coming out of his shell."

There was one memory he didn't want to know the truth about. He had a fear it might have been a premonition. They were visiting his grandparents in New York. After dinner the night they arrived, his parents and grandparents were sitting in the living room talking. Dylan was playing on the floor with a red rubber dump truck his Grandpa had given him. He could still smell that sour rubber as he recalled the memory.

The adults' conversation changed. What had been almost pleasant to listen to, took a dark turn and Dylan became afraid.

"They're just not our kind of people," Grandma said. "Didn't you see their house when you drove up, Howard? It's across the street, two houses down."

"I guess I wasn't paying attention," Daddy said.

"You mean the one with the car up on blocks in front?" Mamma asked. "Yeah, I saw it. Not too good for the neighborhood."

"There's garbage all over that lot," Grandma went on, "They're allowing the place to go to pot. The paint is peeling off, the gutter is hanging loose, and broken windows are patched with cardboard. The children run around like wild Indians, leaving their broken toys all over the place. The parents treat them so poorly, they're growing up to be trash."

Grandma was upset.

"Gertrude, don't get on your high horse," Grandpa told Grandma.

Dylan didn't get that at all. He thought maybe his grandfather was afraid she might go attack the little Indians on horseback the way the cavalry did on TV.

He didn't get much more out of the conversation except that the women sounded fearful and the men tried to make them feel better or get them to shut up. What he did know was to be afraid of the bad family across the street.

During the week of the visit with his grandparents Dylan tried not to look at the bad family's house, but on the last day as they were packing the car to take the long drive home, his curiosity got the better of him and he snuck a peek . . . and then had a long, hard look because he couldn't believe what he was seeing.

There was the car in pieces within the fenced in yard, the run down house gone gray and dirty from lack of care. But the worst of all—the unforgivable and unforgettable—was the small child lying dead in the garbage can beside the curb. Who were these people to treat a child, perhaps their very own, so cruelly? And to leave it on the street where everyone could see it.

No, it can't be, Dylan thought. Must just look like a child. It's trash; softball for a head, wadded, stained towel for a body, arms and legs made of sticks and old rope.

Before Dylan could confirm this, his mother called him over to have his face cleaned. He hated it when she wet her handkerchief with spit and wiped at a spot of jelly or dried run of snot on his face. But this time he was too busy thinking about what he'd seen.

If it was a dead child, then people who saw it, his parents, grandparents, people walking by on the sidewalk, would be outraged and call the police. Unless they were all afraid, scared if they let on they knew about the bad family's crime, they might be killed. This family was so bad even the police were scared of them, otherwise they wouldn't put their dead child out on the street where everyone could see it. Dylan didn't want to anger the family by looking at their dead child, so he kept his eyes turned away.

He wasn't sure why he never said anything to his parents

about it. Was he too embarrassed, or thought they might be, since there wasn't anything anyone was willing to do about it? They got in the car and drove home and Dylan never set eyes on the dead child again.

One day shortly after Ned and his brother Epply arrived in the graveyard, Ned found a way to hurt Dylan. Since here in the graveyard physical pain only came from within, the bully was limited to causing the boy emotional pain. He wasn't smart enough to be any good at it, but Dylan was easy pickings, and Ned, with the blind luck bully's sometimes possess, hit upon the one thing that would make Dylan hurt most.

"You know, my daddy, he's a garbageman," Ned said. "He told me, after you died, your parents tossed you out with the trash. That's how much they cared about you. You were lucky my daddy come along and found you, took pity on you and paid for you to have a decent burial. That's how you ended up here. So you see, little squirt, you owe me."

Dylan never got another look at the dead child in the trash can, but the image was permanently tattooed behind his withered eyes. It had his face now, and whenever he got a glimpse of it, he could feel the hole in his heart grow larger.

There were times when he felt it so keenly he was incapacitated. Lying on the ground, curled into a ball, he'd feel the weight of the universe trying to crush him to nothingness. He'd want to crawl away from the graveyard. Unloved and unremembered, his existence having made no difference in the scheme of things at all, he would end the pain and cease to exist.

If he did end it, would he go to God, he wondered? He wasn't counting on it. His parents had told him he would go to heaven when he died—another one of their lies.

On one of these occasions Ned had given him a swift kick that broke away most of the ribs on his left side. He'd felt lopsided ever since.

Dylan looked down at the baby and felt compassion for it.

He gathered the infant into his arms and gave it a brittle hug, trying not to feel too creeped out. It gripped his thumb in its tiny hand and he experienced a moment in which he absolutely identified with it, almost as if he were trapped behind those wrinkled, permanently sealed eyelids. Imagining that blind existence and always being in worse pain than what he now endured was more than he could bear. He shook the thoughts out of his head.

Seeing the baby's arm bone Jewel had tied back on with honeysuckle had come loose again, he got an idea. Perhaps he could ease into this doing-of-meaningful-things by making small efforts. He set about tying the arm bone back in place.

When he was finished, he looked around for other opportunities, but there wasn't a lot going on in the graveyard and not much needing to be done. He did see he was alone. All but Ned and Epply were following the visitors at a sensible distance at the other end of the graveyard.

Ned emerged from behind the tree, his one remaining eye fixed on Dylan and the baby. He started toward the boy, an overripe smile carving a black streak under his concave nose.

Just this morning Jewel had said to Dylan, "You stick close to as many folks as you can and stay away from the edges of the graveyard 'til we figure out who it is that's up to no good." Realizing he was near the border of the graveyard, Dylan wanted to leave the baby and run away as fast as his little bones would carry him. But he knew he wouldn't get far if Ned really wanted to cause trouble. He stood his ground and looked Ned in the eyes. The bully's swagger seemed to waver ever so briefly. It looked to Dylan as if he'd blinked and glanced away momentarily. That told him Ned was up to no good, but it also gave Dylan courage.

Of all the graveyard inhabitants, Ned and his brother were really his only suspects for the murderer because they were just mean. He didn't like Clay much, but Ned and Epply hurt people for fun.

"Ned," Dylan said, holding the baby closer, "do you know

anything about what happened to Dot and Jim?"

"Do I know? You tell me, little boy?"

Epply stepped out from behind the tree and sidled around to Dylan's left.

"Yeah, I know something about it. It's no big thing. We're just havin' some fun. What's anyone gonna do about it? There's two of us and we're still fresh, still got some heft to us. You and most of the others are just brittle sticks, not even good kindling. Only other fresh one is that Omer, and she hasn't the mind to go up against us."

Epply had come around behind Dylan now. The boy would have called for help but knew his dry, little voice wouldn't carry far enough. He turned toward Epply. "What are you gonna do?"

Epply didn't talk much and this time was no different.

"Jewel said it more than once." Ned lapsed into a mocking high-pitched impression of Jewel's voice. "Damn it, one day I'm going to screw up my courage and leave the graveyard with the baby. I don't guess I should care so much about what happens to me, so long as she goes to her just reward." He and his brother laughed.

Dylan knew what Jewel meant when she said those things— she was upset that no one who'd overcome their fear of the unknown and headed out into the surrounding fields and into the who-knew-what beyond had thought enough to take the baby with them, while everyone knew the infant couldn't make up it's own mind to pass on, let alone crawl more than about ten feet at a stretch, and that only aimlessly. And no doubt Jewel wanted see an end to the pain endured by one who had been here longer than anyone else.

Dylan tightened his grip on the infant. "You're not taking the baby."

"Well, then you're going with it," Epply said.

Dylan stumbled back, his grip loosening as fear of the unknown took hold of him and squeezed. He watched in horror and shame as his arms lifted the baby, offering it to Epply.

"Maybe you should go anyway."

Epply was fast, grabbing the baby with one hand, Dylan by the collar bone with the other. "Now your gonna see how we do it," Epply said as he pivoted and spun in a full circle, picking up speed, holding the two at arm's length. Dylan reached out and held onto the baby. His scream was merely a whistling wheeze. He heard Jewel and Clay call out in alarm from the distance. As Epply began his second revolution, he caught a glimpse of Jewel and Miss Omer running in their direction. At the end of the second revolution, Epply released them. Dylan sailed through the air holding the baby and into Ned's waiting arms at the edge of the graveyard. Ned was ready and pivoted as he caught them, each hand gripping one of them. Dylan could see the plan—Ned would take a couple of spins to increase their speed and then release them when they were aimed toward the field beyond.

Taking a chance of loosing his grip on the baby, Dylan reached up and grabbed Ned's upper arm, just above the elbow. Ned shook his arm as he spun, trying to dislodge his grip. Dylan held on. Finally the bully released them both, but Dylan held on to Ned's arm as well as the baby. Ned spun around one more time as he lost his balance and fell.

Dylan flew to one side and was rising slowly to his feet when Ned grabbed him up and prepared to shove him into the field beyond.

That was when Miss Omer bowled into Ned. When she struck, he dropped Dylan and the baby. There was a loud crack and her head fell away from her body. Her body kept going, driving him into the field and ultimately into oblivion. There was a sound, something like a sharp hiccup, and they were gone, all but Miss Omer's head. A moment later her head rose from the ground and followed in the direction her body had taken.

Dylan turned to see Clay and Jewel menacing the remaining brother. Betty was coming up on his flank. Epply let out a bark of fear and ran into the field after his brother and then he too was gone.

Dylan picked up the baby and moved toward the others.

"Poor Miss Omer," Betty said.

Dylan offered up the baby, but could not meet Jewel's eyes. She inspected the infant for damage. One hand and part of that arm and most of the bones of the other hand were missing.

Dylan wanted to run away, but didn't want the others to think he had something to hide. He was fairly certain they had not seen him offering the baby to Epply.

"Thank you, Dylan. You saved her," Jewel said.

"Yeah, but what for?" he asked, trying to diminish the importance of the event. "You said yourself someone should help it pass on."

"They weren't helping her."

"You were so very brave," Betty said.

"It wasn't anything." Dylan looked at his feet.

"Leave the kid alone, woman," Clay said. "You'll embarrass him." He walked away.

Betty followed him, huffing in disgust. "He might have been killed by those maniacs, Clay. Have a heart."

"That's right," Jewel said. "But we do for each other, don't we Dylan, even when it's a sacrifice?"

The statement was a blade thrust into him and twisted, the pain unbearably intense, but short-lived. This was no butter knife. It pushed through the hole in his heart and exposed an unexplored territory deep inside Dylan.

He found himself lying on the ground. "Are you all right," Jewel asked.

He didn't answer. He was too busy watching her fuss over him, and loving her for it.

"I offered the baby to Epply if he'd leave me alone," he said.

"I saw that. I understand—you were afraid. And you're

right, if they had succeeded, at least she would have passed on."

"If that's all there is to it, why don't you throw the baby into the field?"

"She needs someone to take her there, someone to go with her. I don't know what I'd be throwing her into, and she can't do for herself."

A fresh idea came to Dylan, a frightening one from the new territory that opened inside him. He wanted to turn away from it, but it begged to be explored. Before he could truly experience the terror at the heart of the idea, he acted.

He got up, lifted the baby from the ground where Jewel had placed it and turned to walk out into the field. He told himself not to look back. If he saw Jewel's face, he knew he would want to rush back into her boney embrace.

He hadn't made it far before he felt a hand on his shoulder. When he tried to continue without responding, another hand assisted the first in turning him around.

"Where are you going, Dylan?" Jewel asked as she crouched down to look him in the eye. "What are you doing?"

"I'm taking the baby into the field," he said as casually as he could.

Jewel gazed at him for the longest time, too long. Dylan did and did not want to turn away and continue. There were unknowable consequences ahead.

"Aren't you afraid?" she asked softly.

"Not if I don't have time to think about it. I'm more afraid of not ever doing anything, not meaning anything to anyone or myself. I'm tired of feeling worthless and small. I heard what you said about doing for others."

Jewel's gaze, though fixed on him became distant. Then she shook her head and focussed on him again. "I guess I just say those things and don't mean them or I'd have done what you're doing long ago."

"I have to go . . . or I won't do it," Dylan said, pulling away.

Jewel stood and let him go. Dylan turned and continued with the baby into the field. After a few steps, he felt Jewel beside him and knew she was going with them.

READY OR NOT

A nightmare from my past returns to haunt me, bringing with it the ghost of insanity. I call the ghost Malcolm S. Mulheney, or just plain Mal.

We were best friends in Vietnam during the war. But that was before he killed a couple of my good friends in the jungles of Quang Tri Province. I tried to forget him and the pain he'd shown me. Truth is, I never really got him out of my system and I've never been able to get close to anyone since.

For reasons unclear to me, I have boarded a flight to go see him in the hospital where he's been kept ever since the killings. The flight attendant says something about this airplane being a DC-10 and how he hopes I'll have a good flight. Right now, that's the farthest thing from my mind.

It was what—day before yesterday—I got this call from a doctor named Cutlip at the Tucson V.A. Domiciliary, Mal's home away from home. The doctor asked me what I knew about what happened to him.

"His universe was pulled out from under him," I said. "I told you guys all I knew about Mal back when you owned me."

But the doctor kept talking, telling me he was the new head of psychiatry at the hospital and that, having read all he could on the case, he has some hope for Mal. I didn't want to think about it, but I was polite and I listened.

"You were the one who subdued him when—"

"Hey, I just tackled him," I said. "And the other guys all piled on to keep him from swinging his M-60 around."

"Yes," he agreed. "But it says here in the report that once you got him into the helicopter you kept him calm by talking to him, and that for a short time before he lapsed into catatonia, he was lucid."

He told me that lately Mal has been more responsive to the staff and has been heard to say my name. Cutlip had a whole lot more to say, so I listened, not understanding everything. But I could see the guy had his heart tuned properly, and before I knew it I heard myself agreeing to come visit Mal.

F-15. I locate my seat wedged between a fat man chewing gum with his mouth open and a silly-looking woman wearing too much makeup and fun-in-the-sun apparel. The woman makes little effort to tuck in her legs so I can get by. The fat man has spilled over into my seat. He gives me a look of disgust and lets his breath out sharply as he moves his briefcase and coat so I can sit down. I must not dress and groom myself the way he would like me to. This is typical of the crap I've gotten from people ever since I came back to the States.

I got home from The Nam five years ago and I'm trying to build a life in the real world. It's not much of a life yet— eight jobs in the last three years alone, no good friends and no place to live I'd want to call home. After what happened with Mal it's difficult to trust anyone. I had a girlfriend for a short time, but found myself beating on her and decided to cut the relationship short. I can't seem to get comfortable anywhere or with anyone.

And it looks like I'm not going to get comfortable here either. Damned seat's too small. The fat man and the silly woman are using the arm rests and I have to sit with my elbows in my lap.

As we taxi to the runway, the captain is making garbled noise at us over the intercom.

Smells damned strange in here. Someone ought to come

up with just one perfume to put in all the toiletries for men and women, so if people wanted to stink themselves up like that, at least they'd all smell the same. Then, there'd be none of these weird-ass odor combinations, like the smell of the fat man's hair grease mingling with the five different perfume aromas wafting my way from the five nearest women.

Now that the plane is taking off, I'm stuck with these strangers for the duration of the flight. And they're getting stranger all the time as I breathe their breath and watch their every move.

Some of the smells trigger memories of places and things I'd rather not recall. Remembering the war, I'm becoming more and more uncomfortable with the tightness of my surroundings.

Claustrophobia—I guess this is how Mal felt in the jungle. It was hot and humid, had the most God-awful insects I'd ever seen and the animals screamed at you wherever you went. But to hear Mal talk, it surrounded and touched every inch of him, closed over his mouth and nose and tried to suffocate him.

See, Mal was from Arizona where, he told us, it got hotter than The Nam ever thought of being. "The air's dry, though," he said. "The heat don't follow you around. Even on the worst days, you stand in the shade and you can cool off."

He complained about the jungle getting into his fatigues and boots. I thought he meant the bugs. But he said it was the air itself all full of warm moisture and the smells of the jungle and its people.

He had this nervous habit of swinging his arms and that damned M-60 real wide and shrugging his shoulders for no reason. He'd just be walking along and make these weird gestures like he was checking his elbow room or pushing with his shoulders against the air around him.

He tried to tell me about his claustrophobia—said it started when he was about seven or eight playing a hide-and-seek game called Sardines with some neighborhood friends. I'd never heard of the game myself. He explained that the one who's It hides and the others try to find his hiding place and hide with him. The last to find the hiding place is It for the next round.

When it was his turn, he'd hidden under a rickety loft behind some boxes of newspaper in a rundown garage. Junk was stacked high and carelessly on the rotting frame of two by fours. As the other kids crammed into the narrow hiding place, everything got pushed out of shape, and down came the loft and all this dusty garage shit on top of them.

The other kids got out all right. But Mal was pinned. The framework of the loft had landed on his legs, breaking the left one. A wooden crate on his chest had broken several ribs and punctured a lung. He was fighting for air and at first didn't have the wind to cry for help.

The others were all laughing. Rage and panic overwhelmed him. It was as if he had been swallowed whole and there was no air in the belly of the monster garage. He couldn't move. He felt like if he didn't get out immediately, he would never move again—he would be a fossil embedded in crushing stone, a fossil in terrible pain.

Eventually, he passed out. The other kids finally caught on to what happened and began digging him out of the wreckage. The loft was too heavy for them to lift and they had to find grownups to help. After forty-five minutes, Mal was free, but the terror of that experience would strike him unexpectedly again and again for the rest of his life.

Claustrophobia—I never experienced it until I heard Mal describe it.

Now that we're airborne and the No Smoking light has gone out, the woman to my right lights up. The way she holds her cigarette, the smoke rises straight into my face. She pretends not to notice. I won't say anything, won't give her the satisfaction of knowing I don't like it.

The Sarge wouldn't let anyone smoke while we were out on

patrol. "The enemy can smell it a mile away," he told us.

The game we played in Vietnam was hide-and-seek of the deadly variety. Mal and I were part of a platoon involved in reconnaissance patrols in Quang Tri. Our squad of about eight men hiked deep into enemy territory, counting enemy strengths, directing artillery fire and air strikes and generally collecting information for the brass. We followed the dirt trails that crisscrossed Quang Tri, trails punctuated frequently with booby traps.

The Sarge had us all taking turns on point. When you were leading the way like that, you had to know what to look out for. If you missed just one booby trap, you might find yourself missing a whole lot more. Or it might miss you, and then you'd be missing your good buddy who was walking along behind you.

I remember The Sarge real well—name was Howey Rhodes. He honestly believed in that war, and since I didn't know what to believe and needed a role model, I followed his example.

Besides Mal, I was closest to Blue Boy. He was young and looked like the guy in the painting. He and a guy we called Rampage were the funny ones. The more frightened we were, the harder they tried to get us to laugh.

Spook was quiet. He had this uncanny way of just all of a sudden being there. You wouldn't hear him approach. But you'd turn around and there he'd be. It would startle the shit out of you every time. He was the best at sneaking up on the enemy and he loved doing it.

It's hard to remember some of them, especially the ones that didn't last long—like Igloo. All I remember about him was that he kept all to himself. The guys said it was like he had a wall of ice around him. Others, like Hairball and The Evangelist, an irritating Baptist from Tennessee, weren't around long enough for anyone to get to know them either. Seemed like a core of the squad stayed intact for a long time while our replacements just kept being replaced.

One night we were all bedded down in a small clearing. We knew we wouldn't be hitting the red zone until late the next morning and so we were feeling remotely secure—all but Mal. He wouldn't eat, wouldn't talk to us, just fiddled with his gear, rubbed this photo of his girl (he said this brought him luck) and mumbled to himself. When I looked over at the photo, I could see that her face had been rubbed clean off.

Then, when everyone was asleep but me, the watch and Mal, he turned to me with this look on his face like he'd just shit a poisonous snake and wanted me to help him get rid of it.

"I got fifteen days left, and the closer I get to going back to the world, the more this place crowds me. It's closing in like it's going to hold me down and keep me here. I've got the worst feeling I'm not getting out of here alive—worse than ever."

I didn't need this shit. Everyone was scared of not making it. But it was the way he put it—I could feel what he meant. I'd always had a problem with that; somebody tells me something they feel and it's like I'm right there in their shoes, in their skin, looking out through their eyes. It caused me a lot of pain. Every time I saw someone catch a slug or a piece of shrapnel, it was like I took the impact and the pain along with them. And sharing Mal's anxiety was just the same.

He had been talking like this on and off for some time and it was really getting to me. I wanted to keep my distance, but he was my best friend. We'd survived together.

The next day we were trudging down a trail through a broad, grassy area. I was on point and it had been pretty painless. One bouncing betty was disarmed and we caught sight of a shit-load of pungi sticks before they caught us.

When my turn at point was up, The Sarge tapped Mal on the shoulder and said, "You're It, Mal. Take point."

I fell back and Mal shrugged his way forward. As he passed me, I could see his eyes change, become wide-angle lenses, taking in as much as possible. He might be nuts, I told myself, but he was not likely to miss anything. He was giving himself instructions as he moved along and The Sarge had to remind him to maintain noise discipline. He turned and flashed this fierce look at The Sarge and began to mouth his words silently.

We were approaching a slight rise when Mal saw a bush move. He signaled with his hand and we all dropped. Suddenly, silently, trees on three sides sprouted teenaged boys in tennis shoes, carrying guns to play army. Except these were grown men who looked about the size of fifteen-year-olds to me, and their rifles weren't toys.

Mal took a slug through the upper left arm and Igloo got one in the back. We were all scrambling for the brush. All but Mal, who stood and started pruning the trees with his M-60. The human clippings were falling and he was screaming at them like he knew them by name.

The rest of us were firing and doing our best, but it was Mal who cleaned up. He took another slug in the thigh before he was through with them. But once they were all down, he didn't stop. He turned his rifle on us, nearly cutting The Sarge in two.

I was up now and I tackled Mal. With the wounds he had, he went down easy, but he was still thrashing around, firing his rifle. Blue Boy got one in the head. The others, Spook, Rampage, and a new guy, whose name I don't remember, all grabbed a piece of Mal. Hairball got the M-60 away from him.

And just like that, it was all over and everything was quiet, even Mal. I felt the tension go out of him. His muscles relaxed and tears began to puddle up in his eye sockets as he lay there on his back with his eyes closed.

We called for Med Evac and returned to base. The Sarge, Blue Boy, and Igloo were dead. Mal was packed off to the states and locked away. Two good friends were dead and Mal might as well have been.

I've never known how to feel about it after all these years, much less how I feel about Mal. I do know I'm angry and I want someone to pay for what happened. But I haven't found anyone to pin the blame on, not even Mal.

I get these bizarre urges when I think about it. Like right now, I want to take a rifle and see how many of these passengers I can take out before someone can stop me. There are maybe a couple hundred of them. With them strapped all snug in their seats and me running up and down the aisles with an M-16. . . .

I'm not that nuts, though. Not like Mal.

The captain says we're beginning our descent. That's just how I feel; the closer I get to seeing Mal, the farther I descend into the pit of my angry imagination. Mal made that descent and hit bottom. The difference between him and me is that I'd always been able to pretend it wasn't real, just a bad dream.

But now, reliving some of this shit, I stumble on fears I should have dealt with. They're like the booby traps in the jungle. Instead of denying them, I should have disarmed them long ago.

I know no one is out to get me—that's my rational side—but my feeling is that everyone is out to do me harm. Looking around the plane I can find it in subtle things the people say and do. A lot of the time, it isn't easy to distinguish between what I believe with my rational mind and the crazy ideas that come from what I feel.

I am home from the war and I'm safe. I know it didn't follow me home, but in many ways I feel like it has. The war is in me and I feel shame and guilt for what I've done. I've done the job I was asked to do—a job all of the passengers on this plane counted on me to do—but no one here could accept me if they knew what the job involved. These people don't know that because the squad didn't have the man power to carry wounded prisoners, we shot them in the head rather than leave them behind to alert the enemy to our presence and strength.

I have this fear that it shows in my face, that people can

see I'm a killer, and that one day someone might decide to do something about it. So I'm careful to watch everyone, to see if anyone catches on to who and what I am.

Knowing this is paranoia doesn't help.

So why am I going to see Mal? Fuck, I don't know. Maybe it's because he was my friend and we survived together.

Shit, that's a laugh. Neither one of us survived.

Or maybe I'm partly responsible for what happened to him. I could have made more of an effort to talk to him when he was slipping.

The fat man wants to get by. "The plane has landed, buddy," he growls. "You gonna get off, or what?"

What will happen when I see Mal? Will he give me a big hug? Or is he so nuts he won't even recognize me?

And what about me? In trying to help Mal am I seeking some sort of atonement for whatever it is I think I've done wrong?

"For the most part, Malcolm has been in a catatonic state for the past five years with little response to the staff."

Doctor Lealand Cutlip is a round, red-faced man, kinda nervous and not much like the friendly voice I heard over the phone. His words are as dry and clinical as his office. There isn't anything in here that isn't functional; no gewgaws, art or decorations of any kind, not even curtains, just open blinds letting in the harsh, white Arizona sun.

He's telling me about Mal's condition and there's only so much of it I can understand. His description of catatonia gives me the impression that Mal is holed up inside his own head, trapped in another tight space.

"Periodically," says Cutlip, "Malcolm comes out of it and becomes agitated, even violent. There was an incident shortly after he was brought here in which he attacked an orderly and nearly killed him. And then here recently, he became violent again. An orderly stooped to retrieve a fallen food tray and the sudden movement must have disturbed Malcolm. He brought his knee up into the orderly's face. When the poor fellow reeled back, Malcolm struck him in the throat. If one of our nurses hadn't performed a crude tracheotomy, the man would have died."

"Isn't he locked up? I mean, strapped down or something."

"Oh, no." The doctor is a bit surprised. "That would be cruel. This is not a hospital for the criminally insane and his is not considered a criminal case despite what happened in Vietnam. That was ruled a friendly fire incident."

"So, how can I help?"

"Well, to start with, let's just see if there's any reaction when he sees you."

"But you said he's almost always out of it."

"Oh, he's perfectly aware of everything going on around him. It's just that he's not always able to respond."

The doctor rises, motions toward the door, and we exit the office. In the corridors, there is nothing to excite the human mind. Maybe that's intentional. The light coming through the windows dims. A cloud must be passing in front of the sun.

I hear the echoes of our footsteps, a typewriter clacking, a door opening or closing with a squeak and, far away, a sound halfway between a chuckle and a sob. At an intersection, whispered voices come from the corridor to my right. "He won't be leaving today," is all I can make out.

Are they talking about me? Have they prepared a room for me here?

My palms hurt from my fingernails digging into them. Just take slow, deep breaths. Relax. Cutlip must see how nervous I am. Why doesn't he say anything?

The doctor pauses, his hand resting on the handle of a door. "Malcolm may look very different to you," he says. "He's been inactive for many years."

I nod and my stomach turns a flip.

He opens the door and I see a man leaning against the wall inside the room. An orderly, I guess. Another man sits in a chair, leaning forward as if he's studying the pattern on the tile floor.

It's Mal. But he's gotten so thin. His head is balding, and the little hair left has turned grey. Cutlip motions the orderly over toward Mal.

"Carter, please help Malcolm to sit up."

The orderly crouches and pulls Mal upright. His eyes look vacant. My gut is full of restless worms and my skin prickles all over.

"Position yourself in front of Malcolm," Cutlip tells me, "so he can see you."

Now, face to face with Mal, I see no recognition in his eyes. His face remains slack. Slowly, his eyes focus on me, a slight tremor runs through him and a wet sound comes from his open mouth. I want to hide. His face twists into a childish look of pain, as if he's going to cry. My name comes crackling out of his throat and he begins to reach for me. I shrink away and the orderly pulls Mal back by the shoulders.

His face quakes with anger and Mal drives his right elbow back into the orderly's ribs. There is an audible crack and the man stumbles back and falls to the floor, holding his chest.

I'm up and headed for the door. Cutlip is moving toward me and we collide, head to head—a hard metallic jolt like an electric shock. And blackness.

I move through it, through the flashing honeycomb patterns in my eyes. I must get out.

I stumble on something—Cutlip on the floor.

Why was he trying to stop me?

I'm through the door and I hear Mal behind me. He's grabbing for my shirt tail. Nowhere to go but straight down the corridor. Doors could lead to dead ends, and windows, no time to get one open.

I'm screaming for help, but I don't see anyone.

An intersection—move to the right—have to make it to the stairs.

Mal is screaming now. Looking back, I see him bounce off the wall, miss a step and stumble. But he's on his feet and still coming.

I grab a door frame and swing into the stairway and I'm moving down the winding steps, taking three and four at a time. Above me, I see Mal spring over the railing and drop an entire flight.

I hit the stairway door hard, stunning my left arm and shoulder. But I'm out and I see people and I'm shouting for help.

The door behind me slams open against the wall and I turn and there's Mal with a hungry look on his face and he's coming on with incredible speed. I turn away and run right into an orderly, knocking him on his ass.

And there's the admissions desk and the front door.

Somebody shouts. Looking back, I see that the orderly on the floor has grabbed Mal by the leg. Mal punches him in the side of the head and the man slumps. Another orderly rushes to intercept him. Mal sweeps the guy's legs out from under him and the man goes down with a crack as his head meets the floor.

I'm out the front door and running across the courtyard toward the front gate. Reaching it, I turn to see Mal burst out of the building. With his long legs, he's faster—I'm just across the road and he's already at the gate.

There's nowhere to go—just a plowed field. Beyond the field are trees. I could hide among the trees, or climb one and defend myself from higher up.

The plowed dirt is loose. I can't get my footing—like running in a dream—I can't seem to get anywhere. I stumble over the clods and soft spots.

He's right behind me. I feel his finger tips, his breath.

My heart is a tight, cramping fist, lungs dry and raw and my vision swims.

My foot catches between heavy clumps and I go down. The dirt bites into me. I know what's coming, have to turn over and face him.

But now it's difficult to move. The limp arms and legs of Dr. Cutlip are tangled about my own. Struggling, I turn to see the orderly just beginning to rise, his arms cradling his injured ribs.

A shaft of sunlight breaks free from the clouds and spills in through the window, illuminating the dark form closing in on me.

Shaking the honeycomb pattern from my throbbing, aching head, I look up at Mal. The glow, the relief and sanity that shines from his face is the final insult.

He raises a pale, boney hand. He reaches down and taps me gently on the shoulder.

"You're it," he says.

The world does not approach as it surrounds and suffocates. I am conscious and aware of my surroundings, but I cannot speak and my body won't respond.

NAKED FROM THE GRAVE

with Mark Roland

"How are you getting along with the Mortlow women?" Dr. Richard Harper asked around his cigar. "I know it can't be easy to have your wife's sister and her daughter living with you."

Dr. Wendell Martin did not want to talk about it. He settled into his chair and rolled his cigar between his fingers. The two men were sitting in the office behind the anatomical theater awaiting a delivery.

"Penelope is always a delight. Her sister, Charlotte," Martin took a deep breath, "I mean to have out of my house at the earliest opportunity. Amelia could stay if circumstances allowed." He immediately regretted his tone.

Martin's new wife, Penelope, had swept him off his feet. At forty-five years of age, he had not believed that any woman would truly want him. Their whirlwind romance had lasted less than a month before he knew he must marry her. Within a month her sister, Charlotte, whom Martin had not met, was charged with insurance fraud and murder. Charlotte's husband, Malcolm, had stumbled out of their home on fire and collapsed dead in the street with a stomach full of acid used in his profession as a photographer. When Charlotte tried to claim the ten-thousand dollar life insurance policy she'd drawn on the man, the insurance company asked the local authorities to arrest her. Because her previous husband, also heavily insured, had likewise died under suspicious circumstances, she was tak-

46

en into custody by the local sheriff. Martin was unaware of the death of the previous husband when Penelope persuaded him to post bond for her sister and take Charlotte and her daughter, Amelia, into their home.

Martin softened his tone. "Amelia is a sweet young girl. If it weren't for the presence of her mother, life at home would be idyllic."

Dr. Harper looked under his brow at Martin. "And yet, after less than two months of marriage, you spend your evening with me?"

Harper, a bachelor twenty years his senior, had tried to persuade Martin not to marry Penelope.

"I think it is obvious by now that I am avoiding Charlotte," Martin began impatiently, "Our home is overcrowded with their family heirlooms and curiosities. Charlotte's morbid hoarding of their father's crumbling taxidermy. Her reverence for everything having to do with the man is singular. And her expensive tastes—with my debts and posting bond, I am nearly penniless. I've tried to find them affordable lodgings to rent, but Penelope has rejected every one. We have had bitter words over it more than once."

Dr. Harper said nothing and finally Martin filled the silence. "Charlotte's wardrobe is entirely from the mourning clothier. I became aware of this when her effects were delivered to our house. In all their numerous family photos both Penelope and her sister wear black. I pointed one out that I knew to be five years old and asked Charlotte what they were mourning. She said, 'A nation that has passed away.' She's referring to the war! That was over ten years ago."

"You come from the North. You don't know what it means to us," Dr. Harper said with a dismissive gesture that broke the ash from the end of his cigar. "You said their father was a well-respected judge and that they were well-to-do."

"Yes," Martin said, lost in thought. "Then, with the war, they lost everything but their social standing. They suffered through the siege of Vicksburg. I know that was a horror for the two of them. Perhaps it took a toll on Charlotte's mind. If it weren't for the insurance—" He cut himself off with a look of embarrassment and looked to his colleague.

Harper smiled warmly and said, "It goes without saying that many, many suffered."

"Whatever her experiences, Charlotte is a termagant. I have been able to retain my composure during her spells of rambling and desultory complaint, but it wears on me. If I were not honor-bound to take her in. . . ."

He paused to draw on his cigar, then blew the smoke out quickly as he returned to his rant. "Charlotte is a bad influence on Penelope. She is strong-headed, petulant and fatuous. She takes her position as older sister too far, commanding Penelope much of the time and browbeating her when they are at odds. There are times after I know they have been conversing that Penelope says things to me that are impertinent and result in arguments. I know these are moments when she is in fact angry with Charlotte for her abuse. Of course she always makes it up to me and returns to being a most considerate spouse, but I am concerned about continued exposure."

"You said Penelope lived with Charlotte all her life," Harper said, "except for the time when you first met."

"Yes, so I suppose if her sister was capable of changing her, Penelope wouldn't be who she is today."

Martin paused, reflecting on recent events. "The two are as different as night and day. Just yesterday Penelope was terrified by a finch that found its way into the kitchen. As she cowered in the corner by the ice box, she pleaded with me to help the poor creature get out. Amelia helped me catch the bird in a pillow slip. Then bright-eyed with wonder at the little creature, she asked if she could keep it as a pet. I told her that captivity would surely kill it and she released it through a window. Sweet girl, that Amelia. Much more like Penelope than her mother."

There was another pause. "But I was speaking of Penelope,

wasn't I, her gentle heart and delicate sensibilities? She was not present when Charlotte's husband died and I'm sure she knows no more than I do about this insurance business."

"And Charlotte?" Harper asked.

"I do believe she committed the crime, but I cannot say as much to Penelope for she does so love her sister. The situation is delicate and I hope for a swift resolution. The trial is not until October. Because of their father, they have the best lawyers. I would not be surprised if she is acquitted. If so, she and Amelia must find other lodging immediately. If she goes to prison, we will of course take care of Amelia. Whatever the case, I must trust that when all is done, justice will prevail."

"I just hope you will still be above ground."

"Surely you don't think—"

"I don't want to think . . ." Harper's voice trailed off as he looked at the glowing end of his cigar. "For your sake, October cannot come soon enough."

"Try not to worry. I am determined to have Charlotte out of our lives as soon as possible."

As the conversation withered, a gentle knocking came from the back door of the Anatomical Theater. Their delivery had arrived.

The dim, flickering gas lights gave the impression the corpse was moving ever so slightly, but Martin, Harper and Emmit conversed amiably. *They all wear the same expression*, Martin thought as he looked at the body of the elderly black man sprawled on the table. The blue-gray features, with their gaping, toothless mouth and open, clouded eyes fixed on eternity, held the grim resolve of death. Martin had seen a lot of it and worse as a surgeon in the Federal Army during the war before settling here in Tennessee and taking up a position at the Medical School.

"Just in time for the demonstration tomorrow," Martin

said to Emmit, a thin, middle-aged black man. "He's muddy, but I'll get him cleaned up."

"Ben don't care 'bout no dirt," Emmit said, talking about the man as if he were still alive. "He willing to lend a helping hand, only now he lending both hands an' all the rest too." As if he knew he'd taken the joke too far, he lowered his eyes.

Harper produced a forced smile. "He assuredly will be helping more people this way than moldering in the grave," he said. "Fortuitous to us, but sad for his poor wife that she spent their hard-earned money to have him embalmed."

"Let her think he lyin' in the groun' uncorrupt'ble," Emmit said. "It give her comfort just the same, so long she don' know 'bout this here."

Martin counted out five coins before placing them in Emmit's hand. "Good work, but you be sure to stay clear of that Bennyworth. He's not like the other constables no matter what you say. Sure he talks friendly, but ever since Dolittle snatched his Mother—"

"Bennyworth knows what ghosts as does this resurrectionist's biddin'. He don't got no truck wit' me. Don't you worry." Emmit winked comically.

Although certain Emmit would decline, he asked "Will you stay and have a drop of brandy?"

Emmit glanced at the other physician. Harper turned away. "Much obliged Dr. Martin, but I should be goin'. Got chores early t'morrow morning y'know. Thank you too, Dr. Harper. I'll keep my ears open. You hear anythin', you let me know and I'll get right to it."

After seeing Emmit to the door, Martin helped Harper lift the corpse into place on a table with a V-shaped slate top.

"You only encourage his sort treating them like gentlemen," Harper said. "We've both had enough experience to know we're all bright red on the inside, but it's the man on the outside that matters. Respect starts with self-respect, something of which the black man is incapable."

"Emmit serves us at no small risk to life and limb. To show a little respect does not diminish us and sets a good example. He too is one of God's children."

"Believe what you wish, but you heard; he believes he stands in good stead with evil spirits."

"He jokes about that."

"That's not what I've heard," Harper said. "Wendell, you've been swindled too many times in your business dealings to continue to think you are a good judge of character. You see the good in others, even when it's absent. But enough about that."

Martin forgave Harper his patronizing tone, for the man was twenty years his senior.

"I should be home, Wendell. Please notify our students so we can begin tomorrow."

Martin stood to see the man out, but made no move toward the door. "I'll send word," he said.

"Aren't you coming?"

"No, I have work."

Harper gave him another look under his brow, but then turned and left the room and the building.

Martin was grateful to have the excuse of work that would keep him from returning home until after Charlotte turned in for the night.

He finished his work and was leaving the anatomical theatre by the rear door when he discovered the gris-gris bag, a voodoo charm, tied to the knob. He assumed Emmit was responsible. Stung by Harper's words, he removed the bag and dumped its contents, bits of fingernail and ash, into the gutter.

As the students filed in and took their seats, their whispered jeers reached Martin's ears. "I wonder if we'll have a turn with his sister-in law, after they hang her?" one of them said. Muffled laughter and a few snickers followed. Martin heard the remark just as he approached the cadaver and his head filled with the reek of formaldehyde. The student's question and the smell conspired to create a vision of Charlotte's corpse on the table, her neck broken and bruised, viscera and proper pale skin exposed to strangers. He was disgusted with himself for taking delight in the image. Despite everything she had done, it struck him as a punishment beyond proportion to her crimes. Considering his views of body snatching as a necessary evil, these feelings were an acid irritating the lining of his complacency. It is for the greater good, he frequently reminded himself, but from time to time, he saw himself no less an outlaw than an arsonist or a pickpocket.

Most students became ashen and obviously disturbed by their first encounter with the dead, but there were always those who, needing to deny their disquiet, made blustering jokes or indecent remarks. Martin was grateful to have Harper here to establish order in the anatomical theatre. Martin had never been good at shouting down the rowdies. Harper enjoyed being present to experience what he had largely been denied during his medical training; dissection of a human cadaver. Only recently had the Tennessee State legislature passed laws to remove the criminality of body snatching. With specificity, they determined that the value in a burial lay in the possessions of the deceased, not the corpse itself. As long as the body was hauled naked from the grave, the most a resurrectionist was charged with was trespassing. In this manner, they had paved the way for sufficient cadavers to make it to the medical schools. Martin had heard rumors that Emmit took valuables from the grave, but hoped this wasn't true.

Harper was still trying to establish order in the anatomical theatre when Penelope walked in and there was sudden silence in the room. She moved down the steep steps to take a seat on the first level, mere feet from the dead body.

This took the wind out of Martin. Regaining his composure, he realized she was unfazed by the presence of the corpse. She smiled prettily for him, then gazed dispassionately at the remains on the table. This stood in sharp contrast with the picture he had painted of her for Harper last night. Harper turned to Martin with a questioning look. Martin shrugged, cleared his throat, and bent over the cadaver.

"There are a few boney landmarks I have marked," he began haltingly. "At this time, you can . . . palpate these on your own body as I review them."

He paused as he pictured Penelope palpating these areas on her body while the students looked on.

"Doctor?" Harper said, and Martin resumed his demonstration.

"We'll start with the clavicles and the sternal notch between them. From there, run your finger down the body of the sternum and palpate the point of cartilage called the xiphoid process. I've marked this as well as the margin of the rib cage here and here," he said, gesturing. "Finally, in the area of the pelvis, there are two boney prominences called the anterior superior iliac spines."

Before cutting into the corpse, Martin glanced quickly at his wife. Perhaps Penelope saw much worse in the siege of Vicksburg. *I should not worry for her*, he decided.

"Our first incision will extend from the sternal notch along the sternum to the xiphoid process. The pressure here is not critical because the bone presents a barrier to protect the tissues within. As I continue below the xiphoid process, I'm careful not to cut deeper than the bone allowed me to cut over the sternum so that I do not penetrate into the abdominal cavity."

As the dissection continued, exposing more of the tissues of the cadaver, Penelope gazed on as dispassionately as ever. When her face was without expression, Martin could see the resemblance to her sister, Charlotte. But how could the two be so different?

Last night Charlotte was awake when he returned. He couldn't help thinking how vulnerable he was to her when he was asleep. He was privately horrified when Charlotte offered him a cup of tea, thinking of the contents of her late husband's stomach. He declined saying that he had trouble sleeping. While Penelope hurried to prepare a cup of warm milk to help him sleep, Charlotte disparaged Martin's dealings with Emmit.

"I can smell that man on you," she said without looking at him as they sat in the parlour. "He is the lowest of the low, a dealer in death, and no matter how you justify it, it rubs off on you."

The pot calling the kettle black, Martin thought.

Despite the late hour, Amelia sat next to her, occasionally giving Martin a brilliant smile. Each time, Charlotte smacked her on the wrist.

"It may be that he deals in dead things," he said patiently. "But he and his kind have few opportunities to make a living. The cadavers do no end of good in the education of young physicians. His hauling of animal carcasses to the glue works is hard work few others want."

"I understand he eats those dead animals and would the cadavers as well if you didn't pay so dearly for them." Her voice was deep with disgust. "In winter, he's a bone-grubber, going door to door. There is nothing of death that he will turn away from."

Martin didn't respond in the hope that she would relent.

"And do you know what he does with all that bone and ash?" she asked. "You should ask Tandey."

Martin's black housemaid, Tandey, was a superstitious young woman. Once she warned Penelope not to walk alone along High Street where it passed beside a wood. "There's feral dogs in there. I know a girl had a litter o' puppies after they had their way wit' her."

Martin believed Emmit had an undeserved infamy. Rumor had it he engaged in Burking, the process named after the Scottish criminal, William Burke, who, working with William Hare, strangled innocent victims and sold their bodies to medical schools. Burke and Hare hung for their crimes. Martin didn't believe Emmit capable of this, but to hear Tandey tell it, Emmit's tale was full of murder, dark mischief and hoodoo.

"Doctor?" Harper said again, breaking Martin from his reverie. The demonstration continued.

When time came to break for lunch, Martin asked Penelope what inspired her to come to the anatomical theatre.

"I prepared a special midday meal. I insist you come home to enjoy it." She smiled her most charming smile. "Then we can spend a leisurely afternoon playing horseshoes." Martin knew he was incapable of focusing under her watchful gaze, and there was nothing he could not put off until the next day. Dr. Harper said he would continue the demonstration and that certain boisterous students would take care of clean up and storage. Martin sent for his carriage, and they headed for home.

Martin had a vague recollection of being pronounced dead, but trying to focus on the event was difficult. More curious than concerned, he wondered if this were true. He was feeling no discomfort. To the contrary, he had never felt so at peace with himself. He couldn't move or open his eyes, but felt his limbs being moved around. He heard indistinct voices, sweet voices, coming to him more clearly by the moment, and a beautiful light penetrated his eyelids.

A voice too muffled to identify said, "Open his eyes," and a shadow approached. A warm hand touched his face, and, as his eyes were opened, he felt a tightness in his chest as exhilaration seized him and he wondered if he were about to see the heavenly host.

"Did he move?" The voice sounded somewhat familiar. The hand retreated and the shadow moved from his line of sight.

"Of course not," came another voice.

Martin expected bright angels and heavenly light, but instead made out the blurred forms of two women in black, his wife and her sister Charlotte.

All elation gone in an instant, he thought. *Am I dreaming . . . or . . . am I ill?* He tried to say it, but nothing came out.

"Straighten his collar, Penelope. The photographer will be here soon."

Penelope tugged impatiently on his collar. "This is an absurdity!"

"He'll be in the ground tomorrow. We'll need to show that we've honored him in some fashion. Memorial Tintype is more economical than embalming and a marble monument."

I am dead!

Have I been denied Heaven?

Am I a ghost?

Martin tried to break free from his body, to move through the room without it, but still he was a prisoner. *Am I bound to this body?* He pictured himself, his consciousness shackled to his corpse in the grave, feeling the worms devouring his flesh.

"My marriage is but two months old," Penelope said, her voice rising. "The ink is barely dry on the indemnity."

My sweet wife . . . she has . . . murdered me! They are photographing my dead body. Martin tried again to move. *I don't want to be here—don't want to see them.* He concentrated on merely shutting his eyes, but to no avail.

"Regrets do no good," Charlotte barked. "Doctor Jenkins is beyond reproach. He was father's physician, after all. He's given the cause of death on the certificate as heart failure. We need the money. It was Wendell or Amelia. You agreed to this."

Where is Amelia? Safe at school? I must help her. Martin put every ounce of energy into moving. The room swam before his eyes and he felt sick.

"Is it Emmit you're truly worried about?" she asked scornfully. "You said he was reluctant."

Emmit too?

"He said Tandey was wrong, he had no poison that left no

trace. I told him he would find us what we needed or a resurrectionist would be digging him up, and we'd find someone else to provide the poison. Still."

"You are a mooncalf if you believe anyone would prefer his truth over ours."

Is it poison or dark magic?

Their voices were less distinct and Martin's thoughts less focused.

"I do trust you, dear sister," Penelope said, "but this has been a distasteful undertaking. Every time I shared his bed or listened to his tedious chattering, I remembered that you had made the sacrifice twice already and that it was my turn. I know and accept my duty. However, it didn't make it easier to endure that Yankee's touch."

I loved her in my own way, he thought, as darkness gathered in his vision.

"What matters," Charlotte said, her voice retreating, "is that you are rid of the man and we will be considerably. . . ."

But Penelope's affection was a sham.

The darkening silhouettes of the women fussed about the room as he drifted into unconsciousness. He could only hope this was truly the end. The last thing he remembered was the arrival of the photographer.

There was a bitter taste in Martin's mouth and someone was pinching his cheeks. He aspirated whatever was in his mouth and began to cough. Despite this and the thick smell of clay and soil, the air was sweet, the stars in the night sky still distant and unknowable. There was movement within the earthen pit above and a gritty hand gently covered his mouth to stifle the sound of coughing.

"Do as I say, Dr. Martin," Emmit's voice whispered. "Lie still an' hold your tongue." Martin's impulse was to be afraid of him, but at the same time he knew he was still alive because of Emmit. He couldn't reason out the man's role in all of this. Thinking about what his wife and her sister had done, he couldn't decide whether he'd rather live or die. As his senses returned, his body screamed for more life, while his emotional being retreated from life in shame and loathing.

"Bennyworth's jus' beyon' the gate, so we got to be quiet." Emmit brushed soil from Martin's face, then reached under his arms and lifted him out through the broken coffin lid and into the dirt.

Within moments, he was in the back of Emmit's buckboard, naked under a rough piece of burlap. As they began to move, Martin watched the light of stars appear between and disappear behind moving shadows of trees.

"I could not go against them," came Emmit's whispered voice. "I believe you know that."

Martin thought about Emmit's situation and understood.

"I apologize, Dr. Martin. The only way I could fix it was to have you dead and buried in their minds."

Emmit seemed less concerned with their pursuer now.

"I got me a potion can put a man in a sleep like death—no breath, no heartbeat. Give him a bit more, he your slave for life and think he's dead. My sister in Haiti cook it up from puffer fish an' toad. Under the spell, you got no breath, no heartbeat. Still, had to get to you quick 'fore you come back. Air in that box don't last long. The remedy tastes bad, but it'll make you right again."

"Thank you," Martin said, his voice hoarse. "I thought you were part of it."

"No sir."

"I should have known."

"You have to decide what you gonna do. You can stay dead an' leave town, or take 'em on."

The Mortlows had the weight of reputation and authority. Presently Martin had no strength for such a fight.

"I can take you to the train station. Got some clothes—

nothing fancy—and some money. Let 'em think you's dead. When you's fit again, then decide."

"Yes." Martin could see himself running in shame for the rest of his life, starting anew where no one would know about his marriage to Penelope Mortlow. But he could not help but think of poor Amelia.

He knew he would have to return, and soon.

CREW CUTS

with Troy Guinn

Every hive must have its drones. The facility had The Crew, and it would be agreed, if anyone ever asked, that The Crew excelled at whatever task it was given. These were neither as menial as those of the Manutan, nor as obvious as those of the nurses and orderlies, but the pride of The Crew could be heard in the hum of every light that flickered but never went out and in the wet cough of each machine that shuddered yet still pumped its payload of electric jizz through filthy plastic tubes to a waiting body orifice.

Whenever a problem arose at the facility, a Crew member might be glimpsed running to the rescue, his tool wagon barking and slobbering at his heels. A sharp-eyed spectator at one of Doctor Darling's demonstrations might peer into a dark corner of the surgical theatre and spot a Crew member nestled in the innards of an errant machine, whispering soft gibberish into its smoking valves while another Crewman stood by with a blunt instrument in case the situation got ugly.

Although the Crew was ruthless in its preventative-maintenance, with enough age and experience a piece of equipment might take on a personality of its own, refusing to function as the slave it truly was. A good example of this was the time Doctor Gort's pelvic twister with flailing router rose to its full height and cornered him in his office, demanding two weeks vacation with the his abdominal roach colony implants. The

Crew arrived quickly and with compromises on both sides, the mechanism was soon flailing and twisting away contentedly in its corner. These desperate declarations of self were not always settled so easily, however, and often resulted in riotous disruptions and even the occasional casualty. The Crew was kept very busy.

Each morning, the four members of the Crew disentangled themselves from their secret places within the walls, and arriving one at a time, gathered in the workshop. The drugs they took at night to keep them from shrieking were slow to leave their systems. Once they had adjusted to what passed for day within the facility, they took those chemicals that ensured their maximum efficiency.

"Another day for Mother Pay," Smitty said, giving his customary cheerful greeting as he pushed his massive frame into the crew shop. Rico was hard at work already, under the shop's single amber light. As far as Smitty was concerned, Rico was the Crew's leader, as well as the only true mechanical genius of the four. Smitty envied Rico's classically handsome features; head small and round like a soccer ball, eyes and mouth thin slits above and under wonderfully sporadic mustaches, and dark orange hair which swept two feet straight back from his head to end in a fine point. Lately the big guy had become much more adept at interpreting the grunted commands Rico tossed in his direction, and although they had never made eye contact—Smitty couldn't remember even one time that Rico had glanced up from the instruments he tended—he felt they were becoming good friends.

Smitty could feel something poking at his backside and heaved his bulk to one side of the doorway.

"We could render that," Vess said, painfully twisting a wad of the large man's buttocks, "and have enough grease to keep this facility lubed for a month."

"What then would I have to snack on when I really needed it?" the big guy said, chuckling.

Vess lost his smile. "You're as happy a simpleton as ever pissed on an electric fence."

"Courage and technique. That's all it takes, Vess." Smitty reached out to affectionately pat the Crew member on the shoulder, then aborted the gesture. He had to keep reminding himself to be careful with the man, not only because he could easily crush the small, lean fellow, but because Vess was all sharpness and angles, a living blade who might accidentally put a hole in him.

The two were such opposites that the air fairly crackled between them. Smitty was a being of misplaced goodwill and dumb luck, while Vess, motivated solely by hate, was one searching for that vital point in existence where he might stab out the light of all reality, preferably right between Smitty's moist eyes.

And then, there was the fourth member of the crew, Henbit, who required a breakfast of ten cigarettes before he could even focus his heavily mascaraed eyes or move his lipstick-stuck lips to utter a single sound. He wasn't a Jack, or a Jill, with neither side able to carry the pail of water. Caught in a gender limbo that left him a poor representation of either sex, he had been directed to the facility for surgical intervention, to help him bridge the chasm between Henbit and genderhood.

As a teen, Henbit had been diagnosed as having a chemical imbalance and told he had better settle on a sex or he would surely be insane before he reached thirty. Now, he was in the care of Doctor Simon who secretly knew that Henbit's chemicals were more perfectly balanced than any others known to science, and that he was probably the most sane being on the planet.

Doctor Simon never told the poor creature this. Instead he put him on a truckload of medications and scheduled monthly "sessions." Henbit would emerge from these procedures with genitalia so hungry for the flesh that it fed on itself and rudely smacked its tiny lips. Strangely, he also found that he could no longer pronounce the words *being, by, am, tortured, I, vivisectionist,* and *a.*

Smitty had a crush on Henbit and a particular hope for the sexual choice the creature might eventually make. But he kept this warm, wet secret to himself. He blushed just thinking about it, looking around to see if anyone was watching. That's when it occurred to him that someone was missing—where was Henbit today?

Then an image of his loved one being sucked through a rancid, steaming drain suddenly formed in Smitty's head. "You guys seen Henbit?" he asked.

Rico, tightlipped, stared at the big guy's reflection in a small utility blade.

"I haven't seen it since last night," Vess said.

Smitty spun on his heels and headed for the door.

"Hey, you giant piece of Smit, where are you going? We got work to do."

"I must find Henbit before it's too late!" He exploded through the door.

"I think it's already too late," Vess said, laughing.

Smitty had suspected for some time now that the facility was flushing away some of its employees. Two had recently gone missing and on both occasions, a torrent of water had caved in sections of wall and floor as it cut a path downward through the facility and passed through a great drain in one of the sub-basements.

Smitty prided himself on knowing personally everyone who worked, lived, or otherwise took up space within the structure. When Nurse Vander Knoggin disappeared, he found a shoe on the lip of the drain; one which he recognized as part of the high-heeled pair she wore when she danced on his chest in the facility's annual talent show the month before.

At the time of her disappearance, Smitty brought up his suspicions with the rest of The Crew. Their suggestion was that if he was so worried about it, he had better sit by the drain and be available to prevent another victim.

Smitty started his search for Henbit at the great drain, but found nothing there. By noon, his search had uncovered something unusual several sub-basement levels above. Behind a heap of rusted-out automotive hulks was an abandoned elevator shaft. "This isn't on any of the schematics I've seen," he told his toolwagon as he peered up and down the shaft. The reek of mystery was a sharp tickle on his nose hairs.

He could see that the elevator was now of no use to anyone. One of the steel cables dangled before him and with his powerful arms, he grabbed it and hauled himself upward, leaving his tool wagon whimpering at the bottom of the shaft.

When he reached the top, Smitty found the doors shut tight. He set himself to swinging until he could reach the wall to his left, then kicked out against it with all he had, hurling his massive form across the shaft and bashing a hole through the wall to his right. Pulling himself through the hole, he sent rubble spilling down the shaft with a loud clatter. The tool wagon let out a yelp and disappeared momentarily from sight.

Standing and brushing himself off, Smitty guessed he must be on the highest level of the facility. In both directions, the hallway seemed endless, the gloom only broken by an orange trouble light that would glow for a moment in one spot, wink out and then randomly reappear elsewhere. Wherever the light appeared Smitty could see only wreckage, broken walls, twisted ductwork and shattered furniture.

The heat was stifling and he wiped the sweat from his face. Something fluttered about his head and he closed his eyes, enjoying the slight breeze it made on his moist skin.

In the distance, Smitty could hear rushing water. Pulling his goodwilly wrench from his utility belt, he moved toward the sound.

He turned a corner just as the orange light came on overhead, revealing a figure standing in his path. His surprise at meeting up with someone on this forgotten floor was quickly replaced by confusion as he failed to recognize one who was obviously a surgeon on staff. The doctor was leaning against the wall, his surgical mask pulled down to reveal a lipless, pink mouth housing rows of tiny, needle teeth. He was shaking his head curtly from side to side, as if denying an unspoken accusation.

"Another day for Mother Pay," the big guy said in greeting.

The Doctor remained silent as the light shifted slightly to reveal his blood-soaked gown. Shreds of viscera clung to it here and there, some squirming for a better grip.

"Be sure to put all those back where you found 'em, eh Doc," Smitty said, chuckling.

The light jumped away.

Smitty wished the doctor's black silhouette a good day and continue his quest. In the darkness, his thoughts had nothing to latch onto and drifted back to the last time he had seen Henbit.

The Crew had been in the off-duty lounge having a sustenance break. They were all kneeling around the feeding cavity, spooning out sloppy chunks of nutrient, while headless, grey lounge attendants mechanically tied off their arms for them and administered injections of work enhancer.

Because he thought he had a gift for gab and for getting others to talk, Smitty jabbered away between mouthfuls, searching randomly for that subject which might spark interest and conversation among the others.

"You guys think that wrestler fella will be better in the ring now that he's got that baboon arm?"

Rico turned his spoon so he could see Smitty reflected in its surface and grunted something that no one but the big guy could understand.

"Okay boss," Smitty said, quickly turning back to his meal. Then he dared to make a quick glance over at Henbit, the radiant one, who seemed to glow even in the brutal glare of the lounge lights. Smitty was sure he had never seen the genderless Crew member look so beautiful. The image was rudely shattered when Vess speared Henbit's cigarette with his pinkie and plucked it out of his mouth. Henbit cursed and sputtered smokily.

"Isn't this your day to meet with Doctor Simon?" Vess asked, keeping the cigarette just out of Henbit's reach.

"You know damn good and well it is, Vess. The only reason you bring it up is to piss me off."

"I just thought you might be looking forward to it. I know, at least, a part of you is." Vess followed his remark with a suggestive series of smacking and sucking noises.

Henbit hissed, spraying Vess with nutrient-rich spittle. Then his cherry-glossed lips drew back in a grin. "Simon's the one who's going to suffer today. He'll soil his comfy pants when he hears what me dug up on him."

"Tell us," Smitty said. "What did you find out?"

"Just never you mind, Smittens. Just never you mind."

Henbit poked another cigarette into his mouth. Igniting the Zippo he had recently purchased to light Henbit's cigarettes, Smitty hastily leaned across the others. In the process, he plunged his right elbow into the feeding cavity. Sensing a pause in their meal, the appliance was solidifying the sustenance, and now Smitty found himself hopelessly stuck until the machine ran through its entire cycle once again.

Ignoring Smitty's failed bit of gallantry, Henbit struck a match off the exposed neck bone of a passing lounge attendant and lit his cigarette. "Let's just say we've been doing some talking with Lefty, in Procurement, and there seems to be this certain mysterious connection between Simon and the disappearance of those inflatable torsos and that box of battered chicken parts Darling's been resurrecting Cain over. If Simon's smart, you'll be seeing the new, improved, and dare me say, more beautiful Henbit very soon."

"Gee, that's too bad," Vess said. "Like Smitty, over here, I've grown enamored of your ambiguous delights, particularly when I crouch down here to eat and I get an eyeful of your manly teats wagging through those low-cut blouses you wear."

The yellow trouble light appeared directly overhead, yanking Smitty back to the present.

And that was the last time we were all together, he thought. A tear formed in his eye as he reflected on the camaraderie shared by the Crew.

He continued toward the sound of rushing water, crushing debris beneath his giant feet as well as those things that would rather be stepped on than drag themselves out of his way. The corridor seemed to go on for miles and he was becoming irritated. Sweat was pooling up in his crotch, his head was getting smaller by the minute, and his tiny friends were setting fire to the forest in his armpits. The image of Henbit and the drain haunted him. With his last injection wearing off and patience wearing thin, Smitty's confidence was dissipating. He seemed no nearer to the sound of the water and as time continued to drag on, he began to fear he was going the wrong way. He was debating whether or not to turn back, when a green light spilling from beneath a door caught his attention.

Something that felt like intuitive certainty clambered up his back and beat a savage rhythm on his occipital lobes. He reeled under the assault of unformed hallucinations.

When his vision was returned to him, he adjusted his goodwilly wrench and tried the doorknob. The door opened with an oily hiccup and he stepped inside.

Tiny particles like flakes of dead skin floated down through the gloom, causing Smitty to sneeze. The wall through which he entered and the floor on which he stood disappeared into the particulate haze. From the darkness beyond came a sighing and moaning, as of an immense, weary entity dreaming fitfully. A simple black desk stood before him, a gigantic lava lamp, the source of the green light, sitting atop it. Within the lamp's swampy glow, Smitty watched a fetus-shaped globule break off and float upward. At the lamp's base was a brass plaque that read *Chief Administrator*.

Taking a step toward the lamp, Smitty found his path suddenly blocked by a sweaty, blue-black head with a prehensile proboscis which bore scars characteristic of Doctor Darling's work. The face, although obviously annoyed, bore an expression of intense curiosity as it blasted Smitty with hot breath that smelled not unpleasantly of pond scum. Precariously riding a long oily, bucking bronco of a neck, the head drew back, coiling as if to strike. The big guy cowered down, holding his goodwilly wrench out for protection, but the being merely sniffed cautiously around Smitty's ears and smoking armpits.

"Is that you making so much noise, down below?" it asked, fighting for a better grip on the neck. "Busting stuff up, making a nuisance, upsetting us so."

"Another day for Mother Pay," said Smitty, as if this explained everything. His rubber face beamed. "Hello too, and who are you?"

"Silister," the head spat. "Assistant to the Chief Administrator. Very busy, no time for games."

Smitty stifled a laugh, trying to picture Silister as a secretary, taking dictation and fetching coffee.

"I'm Smitty, of The Crew. I need to speak with the Chief, so's I can fix his little . . . er, problem."

"Problem?" snapped the bouncing head.

"The . . . uh . . . plumbing problem. People's gettin' washed away while they're trying to do their jobs. Now I know the Chief needs my help—I can feel him wantin' and needin'— but maybe he doesn't even know it himself. I'm an empath, you see."

Silister seemed at a loss for words and Smitty continued. "When I was a young 'un I fell into my pappa's cement mixer and jammed it up. When they finally found me, they had to dig me out with a jackhammer. All that pounding on my head and then those aliens that operated on my brain musta knocked somethin' loose. I know it sounds like a crock, but it's true, and I been like this ever since. Ask Nurse Peabody, she knows all about them aliens—although we can't agree on what color they are. Anyway, I can sense emotions, do astral projections—oh, and I time travel, too. So, tell the Chief that Smitty's here to fix the plumbing."

Silister shuddered. "You try to spin web of nonsense to trap me." His snout vibrated angrily. "Chief has no problem. Flushing periodically necessary. Shed dead weight to cut budget—rids excess. No problem."

Smitty gaped. "Excess! But these are important folks we're talking about. You can't just flush Henbit like a worthless turd."

"Henbit." Silister snorted the name and Smitty had to dodge a greenish spray from the creature's elephantine protuberance. "Foul abomination. Was sticking n-n-n-nose where it didn't belong. Excised from internals, quick as that." Somehow Silister caused his nose to snap.

"You're talking about the thing I love," Smitty said, his massive frame swelling and turning an angry red.

Silister giggled. "That thing took it in every hole, at any time, from everyone, except you. Be smart, kid. You dumb big guy, very useful. Others got to go. You keep quiet and increase dosage. Otherwise . . ."

"You mean Rico and Vess? But Rico, he's a real genius with machines, and that hair . . . it would be a shame. And Vess—he's . . . uh . . . well . . . been around for a long time too."

"Don't need long-timers, geniuses. Machines running themselves, now. Feel them humming, singing." Silister's eyes rolled back into his head and, as if chanting a mantra, he whispered, "Budget cuts—shed dead weight, rid excess. Budget cuts—shed dead weight, rid excess."

Smitty saw his chance. He grabbed the neck and brought his goodwilly wrench to bear against Silister's proboscis. The blue-black head lost its grip on the neck and fell, striking the massive lava lamp and knocking it to the edge of the desk. The fetus within was wide-eyed with terror as the lamp teetered, then fell. It shattered into a thousand musical pieces, and the tiny chief administrator, glowing amidst the wreckage, began the wail of the newborn.

Silister rocked back and forth on top of the desk like a turtle on its back, his myriad centipedal legs kicking uselessly in the air. The neck wasted no time in withdrawing from the scene.

"Idiot!" Silister snarled up at Smitty. "Look what you've done. It took forever to climb that thing."

The big guy thought a moment, hoping to come up with something really mean to say. Finally, he said, "You've got a big nose," he said.

Smitty stepped over the fetal chief and found the door. Two steps out into the corridor and he had a plan—if they wouldn't let him fix the plumbing, he'd just have to stop up that big drain in the basement.

Halfway down the corridor he heard Sillister's door burst open, and he whirled around. Water poured from the doorway, rushing toward him and sweeping up everything in its path. It even picked up Smitty, and like some lost beach ball, he tumbled head over heels in the dark and stinking wave.

He cried out as the water carried him around a corner and bore him down another length of hall. Clinging to his good-willy wrench, the big guy clawed with his free hand to pull himself out of the flood. Smitty knew the torrent would round one more corner before tumbling into the elevator shaft, and made a last desperate grasp to anchor himself. He reached for a splintered door, but the ragged wood decided to go with him and they were swept over the lip of the shaft and fell into the darkness.

"I'm coming to join you, Henbit!" His quivering voice was lost in the roar of the water.

As he dropped floor by floor, he could see briefly through

the open doors of the elevator shaft. Wreckage crouched in eternal gloom on the higher floors, but lower down, at the ward levels, he caught glimpses of facility life; a nurse on the floor having sex with a biopsy punch . . . two surgeons wrestling over a bloody piece of something . . . Doctor Darling shooting holes in the walls with a rusted Hugh B. Automatic. Then Smitty almost collided with an orderly who was leaning out into the downpour to wash his hair.

The bottom of the shaft rushed up to meet him. He crashed through it, catching a brief glimpse of his tool wagon as it dropped the rat it was savaging and jumped in after him. Entering the bowels of the facility, Smitty stopped struggling as a thought occurred to him.

"Maybe I'll be big enough to plug up that drain."

In the days that followed Smitty's adventure, the facility hummed and clanked with a new vigor. The mechanical and the organic worked together and performed their functions as never before, as if for the first time guided by a single mind. Suffering was on schedule.

This did not benefit everyone. Rico and Vess, now co-cooned within the feeding cavity, were no longer called upon for their skills. They found that with frequent lubrication of neck bones, the lounge attendants were always ready with a hypodermic.

The water no longer caused its violent disruptions. Instead, a pleasant, clear green stream wound its way down, floor by floor, to the deepest part of the facility. The liquid tickled the handle of a bent goodwilly wrench just before it passed from sight through the massive drain in the floor.

JUST HOW EXPENSIVE A FREE LUNCH CAN BE

with Mark Edwards

It all started with boogers, Velma thought, and she knew it was the truth. She would not be where she was in life without them.

Officer Mann had never placed her in this holding tank before. Dark and moist, the cell was a featureless concrete room with a metal door and hole in the floor. There was no place to sit but the cold, wet floor. Her cell mate, a scrawny, pale white fellow, introduced himself as Ducky Dwayne, then continued to stared off into space disconsolately.

"What are you doing in here?" she asked him.

"When I abuse people with ducks," he said, "I sometimes I kill them."

Velma nodded her head as if she understood.

"I'm not all alone in the world, though," he said, suddenly defensive. "I've kept Gilbert in my back pocket since '79. He's been awfully quiet and I've worried about him, but not enough to take a look."

Velma became curious. "You want me to look?"

"Better not," Ducky said, angrily.

To calm him she offered him some of her lip color. The lipstick was almost gone, and she felt she was generous to offer it.

"No thank you," he said quietly. "Maybe later." Then his expression changed. "If we're still here," he added quietly

"What do you mean, 'still here'?" Velma popped the remaining lip color in her mouth and chewed.

"You know—before the bus."

"What bus?"

"Don't you know why you're in here?'"

"Just like always—a free meal and a place to sleep."

"Oh, no." Ducky nervously fingered the stitching on his back pocket. "We've been separated from the others 'cause they're tired of foolin' with us."

"Foolin' with us?"

"We're on the next bus out to the facility—you know, at St. Blackledge. The police pick you up too many times, they give you a one way ticket outta town. St. Blackledge, 'cause nobody comes back from there. St. Blackledge don't send nobody back."

Officer Mann took Velma and Ducky Dwayne to the bus depot, explaining all the way how generous the city was to buy them both tickets for a vacation in St. Blackledge. Knowing what a nice fellow Officer Mann was, Velma didn't pay much attention to all the fuss Mr. Dwayne made.

As they were about to board the bus, Ducky made one last try. "I ain't gettin' on that bus," He said. "When Gilbert gets car sick, it's awful. People start dropping like bird shit. You want that on your head?"

"You are gettin' on that bus, Ducky," Officer Mann told him. "Don't think you're not. I don't want to have to throw your ass on there."

He tried to make a dash for it, but Officer Mann caught him and shoved him back. Ducky fell, breaking his nose on the bottom step of the bus.

Velma helped him to his feet and led him on board to a seat next to an old man in overalls. He offered Ducky a handkerchief for his bloody nose.

"No thank you," Mr. Dwayne said, coughing wetly. "Maybe later."

Velma watched hungrily as he lapped at his nose gusher, then turned to say goodbye to Officer Mann.

He stood in the doorway scowling. "Shut up Velma and sit down."

The driver climbed aboard, started the engine, then drove out of the depot and into traffic. The bus was about half full, everyone keeping pretty much to themselves throughout the trip.

Ducky was quiet as well and even stayed in his seat when the bus stopped in Earlville. Velma stayed in her seat too, watching the other passengers get off and walk around in the station, some smoking, some buying snacks from the vending machines. She was hungry too, but had no money. That was okay—with such a delicious body as hers, finding something to eat was never hard—the callouses of her feet, the tender flesh of her lips, the dandruff scrapings from off her head.

She was exploring the corners of her eyes when the driver called out, "All aboard!" The only one to return to the bus was the old man who sat next to Ducky.

Traveling from Earlville to St. Blackledge, Velma couldn't help noticing the way the landscape turned from green to grey to black. After the farmland gave out near town the landscape was dominated by factories, warehouses, junkyards, landfills, and the occasional lake of raw sewage, workers eating their lunches along the shores.

Coming into downtown St. Blackledge, Velma wondered about the streetlights being on. It wasn't night time yet, but come to think about it, it sure was getting dark and the lights were needed.

The place had a terrible problem with pollution, she decided as she watched trickles of sooty fluid drooling across the outside surfaces of the windows. The air smelled of paint thinner, marshmallows, burning cat shit, honeysuckle, boiling tar, and baking bread all mixed up, curling the hairs in her nose.

Velma had never seen such ugly buildings. Homes and businesses alike were wet, greasy, and black. Their windows were painted over and their roofs sprouting great tangles of pipes and puffing stacks.

The bus went so fast, Velma couldn't get a good look at the natives, saw nothing but blurry shapes slopping along the sidewalks. She thought some of them looked broken.

When the bus headed up a hill the air did clear a bit. On top there was a tall structure that seemed to Velma like some scary government building or maybe a plant where old things were made. It was so tall and thin, it made her dizzy just to look at it.

The driver must be in a big hurry, she thought as he slung the bus around to the back of the building, throwing gravel. He screeched to a halt on a concrete slab under a large shed and yelled, "End o' the line. Everybody off!"

Velma moved up toward the front, noticing that Ducky was still in his seat. She crouched down to talk to him. The late afternoon light streaming through the greenish windshield lit up Ducky's tucked in shirt and she saw it had filled with the blood oozing from his nose and bulged out like a little pot belly. The red juice was just beginning to seep through the cloth.

"I think he has expired," said the man in overalls.

As the old man got up and left the bus, Velma slid her hand into Mr. Dwayne's back pocket. She was startled when she felt a desperate wiggling in there, then felt something like a kiss on the tip of her finger. *Gilbert?* she wondered. Whatever it was, she realized it was trapped. Velma liked good deeds, so she curled her fingers around the little doughnut-shape and pulled it out.

The bus driver was hurrying her along so she didn't have time to get a look at the thing. She slipped it into her bra for safekeeping and stepped off the bus.

As soon as she was clear, the bus took off, roaring out of

the shed, around the building, and out of sight. Velma and the old man in overalls stood together breathing diesel fumes for a moment and looking around.

The roof of the shed sagged and had a gaping hole in it as well as spots where instead of shingles there were some large nest. Velma looked up through the hole and saw a blue halo circling the upper floors of the building. She wasn't at all certain she wanted to enter the place.

Velma started when orange lights on the nearest wall of the building flashed and a revolving door began to whirl around.

Seeming to sense her fear, Gilbert crawled out of her bra, down her belly, and into her underpants.

A frail, almost skeletal woman dressed in black emerged from the swiftly turning door and approached. She looked the old man up and down and said, "You can go. I don't think we can use you."

The old man turned and walked off toward the distant hills.

"I'm Inquisitor Gunch," she said. "Follow me"

The two entered the building.

"It all started with boogers," Velma said, finally voicing her earlier thought. This realization seemed to hold some significance, but at present she couldn't grasp what it was.

Inquisitor Gunch seemed to perk up at the statement. Dressed like a nurse but all in black, Gunch sat at a desk piled high with paperwork. Velma saw the blood pulsing through the woman's veins pick up speed, then noticed something knocking around inside her bald head. The inquisitor began furiously scribbling a note on the skin of her wrist.

Living on the street, Velma thought she had seen most everything, but never had she met anyone like the inquisitor. Nor had she been anywhere like this before. She glanced around the miserable cubicle, taking in the profusion of cobwebs that rounded off the corners of the room, and the dinner-plate-sized blisters that measled the walls. Some of these blemishes had burst open, and oozed a cloudy yellow serum.

Finally Gunch made a mark on the paper in her clipboard; a check in a box next to a word that was too small and up-side-down for Velma to read, then looked back up at her expectantly.

Velma was tired of all the strange questions, feeling as if with each answer she was giving up bits and pieces of herself, pieces that might not be returned. But that was silly, and after all the woman had promised she would be well fed for her efforts. Velma's stomach growled just thinking about it.

"Could I trouble you for some lip color," she asked the Inquisitor. "I haven't really had a good meal all day."

"If you'll just answer the questions I'll turn you loose in the facility and you can eat anything you can find."

"Well, all right," Velma said with a sigh. "As I was saying, it all started with boogers. Most children give them up with time I suppose, but not me. Strange how people let things like that go to waste. I guess they just don't have a taste for it, or they've never really been hungry. Hell, I'd eat it for them if they didn't get so upset about it."

A creeping smile sniffed around the Inquisitor's eyes and mouth and then fled. Velma wondered briefly what that was all about, but then shrugged inwardly and went on.

"As I grew up, I found my body had all kinds of tasty treats. Fingernails. Scabs. Dead skin. Blood's pretty good, but you gotta watch out or you'll make yourself sick."

"I had a normal enough childhood—you know—working for my mama at home in the double-wide—nothing special. A lot of fetching and cooking for her and her boyfriends she had a lot of those—some chores, a little TV, and all like that.

"Then on my twelfth birthday, I came home and my key wouldn't work. Mama had been threatening to put a new lock on the door. When she wouldn't answer to my knocking, I figured it was her way of telling me I was all grown up and it was time for me to take care of myself.

"It was just as well. She never really did get along with me pickin' my nose and stuff—said it was embarrassing in front of her boyfriends. She had some funny attitudes about personal hygiene.

"I tried working, but I guess I wasn't cut out for that sort of thing. Panhandling and garbage prospecting got me through the years to come."

"When was the last time you had a permanent address?" Gunch asked.

"You mean where I sleep?"

"Yes."

"How could it have an address if it changed all the time? Mostly I just hung out at the arcade, the library, and a few other places in downtown Ephemeral City where I could scrounge a bite to eat or a little spare change."

Gunch made another mark on the paper in her clipboard. "Is there anything else unusual you like to eat?"

"My favorite?"

"Sure."

"Lipstick!" Velma said with a great sloppy smile. "I remember the day I discovered it as clear as if it was yesterday. Summertime. Blinding white sky. I was standing in the street ringing wet with sweat from the heat off the concrete and asphalt. I found the tube lying in the gutter, top off, half-melted bright pink tip sticking out just as pretty as you please. I picked it up, sniffed it, and the smell made me drool.

"I bit off a greasy pink chunk and chewed. It slid all over the inside of my mouth, creamy pink on my gums and teeth. I could almost taste the color."

Velma paused, her thoughts far away. Gunch arched an eyebrow, stretching the tissue around her eye socket until the bone of her skull showed white through the skin.

"After that I couldn't get enough of the stuff. About a

week later I was arrested for shoplifting. It was officer Mann who caught me with my pockets spilling over with lipstick. He let me go with a warning, but I got so I was pretty good at keeping myself in lipstick without being caught."

"Now isn't that interesting," the Inquisitor said, the glint in her eye that of a black hole. "Doctor Simon will want to hear about this immediately. You wait here and I'll be right back."

Velma thought the woman was going to get up and leave, but instead Gunch sat up straight and her eyes went wide and glassy. Velma became uncomfortable in the silence that followed and tried to think of something to say.

"I've never been out of Ephemeral City before, and it scared me to get off the bus and look up at this big building. I don't know if you're aware of it, ma'am, but there's this weird blue light circles the top floors. Somebody ought to fix that. I wasn't at all sure I wanted to come in here—creepy."

Velma made a lopsided face with bugged eyes and inverted lips.

"Then those grimy orange lights on the wall began to flash and the revolving door started turning. I was about to turn around and go home. But then you came out and everything was fine—remember?"

Although Velma smiled for the woman, Inquisitor Gunch made no response. She remained motionless, eyes staring forward. Even the blood in her veins seemed to have stopped moving, and there was no longer any motion inside her head. Velma reached out to tap her on the arm. It felt like stiff rubber, not at all lifelike. Velma pinch up a bit of Gunch's forearm and then let it go. The waxy grey material sluggishly settled back down.

"Why, she's not even real."

The Inquisitor blinked, and spat out a tooth. It landed in Velma's lap. "I'm back," said Gunch. "I have a few more questions and then the doctor would like to see you in his office."

Velma remembered her mother talking about an epileptic

cousin of hers. 'Fits' and 'spells.' That's what Mamma called what Gertrude had. Gunch must've just had a 'fit.'"

Gunch looked down at the page in her clipboard. "Do you have any family or friends still living?"

"Well, I don't suppose they'd be friends if they weren't still alive."

"Well, do you?"

"Well, yes," Velma said indignantly. "I mean, no—not alive."

"Fine." Gunch made a mark on her clipboard.

"Is there anyone who knows where you are at this time?"

"Well, there's you and the police who sent me here."

Gunch smiled with forced patience. "No one else?"

"There's Gilbert."

"Who's Gilbert?"

"Why he's the little one who lives in my pants."

The Inquisitor rolled her eyes and made another mark. "You've talked about an Officer Mann—was that your only experience with the police?"

"Oh no. Officer Mann used to haul me down to the jail quite regular to get a meal and a good night's sleep. He pretended to be angry with me every time he picked me up. I guess that's what they have to do even when they're doing something nice like that."

"Would anyone really care if you were living or dead?"

"Well, of course they would. No one would talk to me, or say, dance with me or anything like that if I was dead!"

"Okay, I get the picture."

The inquisitor made a final check mark and stood. Velma offered her the tooth. Gunch took it and popped it back into her mouth. "This way please," she said, motioning toward the door.

Velma was led down an exceedingly thin and dusty hall to another, much larger room and told to wait there for the doctor. She entertained herself by examining the collection of antique medical instruments on display in the smudged glass cabinets along the walls. Although wired into position and with museum-like labeling, several of them seemed as if they had just returned from surgery. Gore puddled beneath a saw and beaded wetly on a couple of knives.

Velma turned away from the cabinet and sat in a chair which was bolted to the floor in the center of the room. She had just remembered the loose scab on the cut on her elbow when she looked up and there was someone hovering over her.

"Hello," he said, "I'm Doctor Simon." There was a cage over his mouth and the voice coming through the bars was tiny and insubstantial. He wore a bonnet and a monocular device on his left eye which emitted a greenish-yellow light. "I hope you haven't been waiting long, sweetie."

He looks kind of strange, but he's very friendly. I wonder what he's hiding behind his back. Maybe it's a present.

"What's wrong, honey pie," he said, "cat got your tongue?"

"No," Velma said, "not too long I guess. Have you got anything to eat, Doctor? I've chewed all my fingernails down to the quick and I'm feeling whoosy from all the blood."

"Oh yes, my dear—there's plenty to eat."

When he smiled, the cage stretching with his lips and the bars spreading a little, Velma could see something not at all tongue-like moving around inside his mouth. That was kind of weird, but if they were going to feed her, she could put up with a lot—she always had.

"Yes siree—you'll do nicely." Simon winked at her. "What we would like you to do is to participate in a little food study. Doesn't that sound nice?"

Where were his legs? His uniform, or whatever those long black strips of cloth were supposed to be, fell almost to the floor and were constantly in motion, but his legs were not to be seen among them.

"Does it pay?"

"You are so cute. But to answer your question—no, there's no pay, but you'll have all you can eat for the rest of your life for free."

Velma grinned uneasily. "That sounds nice."

When Simon smiled again, she saw what looked like little hands grasping the bars of the cage. She heard the tiny voice suddenly change its tone and call out, "Help me!" Simon snapped his mouth shut and chewed.

When he opened it again, nothing came out at first. Then a broken, weaker version of the voice said, "What do you say, Velma dear?"

This was really creepy. Velma squirmed in her seat wondering if she should get out of here. But as odd as he was, the doctor's smile was warm and friendly.

Velma decided she should at least look around the facility and get a feel of the place before she committed herself to anything. She started to get up. "I think I had bet—"

Fast as cobras, Simon's hands swung out from behind his back. They struck Velma with tiny steel teeth and injected their venom.

The voice, still not completely recovered, spoke again. "There now, we'll have you processed and fully operative by the time you awaken."

Simon dropped the spent syringes and the world swung out of view.

At first Velma found her situation quite tolerable. Naked, she lay on her right side on a stone slab, bolted in place by a series of expandable steel straps. She wasn't free to move around and that was an inconvenience, but then where had she been going with her life anyway?

The good part was that she was never hungry. A big iron hopper loaded with what the staff called, placenta, was attached to one edge of the slab and a somewhat flexible, yet sturdy copper tube ran from it right down her throat and into her stomach. Gravity forced the substance into her system at a constant rate. Periodically someone came by to hose her off between the legs.

Velma couldn't actually taste the placenta unless it got backed up and gurgled up through her throat and into her mouth, but the soothing aroma was always there, rising from her gullet to fill her head.

"What a pretty name, placenta," she said around the tube. The words came out all garbled and she tried again. "Placenta, placenta, placenta. . . ." she said over and over until she could pronounce it clearly around the tube.

Velma relaxed and allowed herself to be lulled to sleep much of the time. Were they putting a drug in her food, she wondered lethargically, or was she so sleepy because she was always full? Oh well—it didn't really matter. They were doctors after all. She was sure they knew what they were doing.

She decided that the slab must roll on wheels, although she never did hear them turning. From the position in which she was confined, Velma couldn't actually see the castors, but the nurses and orderlies were able to easily push her from room to room.

Most of the time, she inhabited a darkened space full of the low rumble of heavy machinery and the flash of strange lights. Out of the corner of her left eye, she could just make out emaciated figures standing in glass tubes, their slack features suggesting a lifeless sleep. Part of another study, no doubt.

As the days passed, she rose more and more frequently out of her repose as snatches of nightmare troubled her sleep. Were they bad dreams or was she actually catching the staff at some foul deed? If nearby when she opened her eyes, the nurses and orderlies, even Doctor Simon, acted suspiciously; as if they barely had time to conceal some mischief they were about. On several occasions, she could've sworn she saw them chucking human body parts into her hopper. At one point it seemed Simon brought in most of an Asian fellow and dropped him in.

Each time she awoke, she was surprised to find she had taken on ten or twenty pounds in body weight. Having been embarrassingly skinny all her life, at first she was not overly concerned.

She got to know Lefty, the half-man from procurement whose job it was to keep the placenta coming. He was pretty ignorant for a medical technician, being unable to answer any questions about the facility, the doctors, or even the study of which she was a part. But the abbreviated fellow was someone to talk to and it allowed her to practice speaking around her tube until she had mastered it.

As Velma grew in size, she became more and more uncomfortable. When she reached three hundred pounds, she decided she would have to say something to the doctor, but it wasn't until she reached six hundred pounds that he finally got around to seeing her again.

She heard a door squeak, strange light streamed into the room, and suddenly there was the doctor smiling down at her.

"Velma, you're looking plump as a peach," said the strange little voice inside Simon's mouth cage. "As a matter of fact, that's what I'll call you from now on. Peaches—isn't that a sweet name?"

I think he's flirting with me. Maybe when this is all over we'll start going out together. He's not the most handsome I've seen, but I could do worse than to marry a professional man.

"Yes," Velma said, "it's very pretty."

"And does my sweet Peaches have all she needs?"

"Oh yes—Lefty says I get to eat Chinese today. I'm not exactly sure what he means by that, but he promised a fifty gallon drum of soy sauce to go with it."

"I'm glad you're enjoying your work."

"Yes, but don't you think I'm being given just a little too much to eat?"

"It's all part of the study, Peaches. Nothing lasts for ever, so enjoy it while you can." He showed her that big smile again and left the room.

Two hundred pounds later, the doctor returned.

Despite the pins and needles of poor circulation in her overburdened limbs, Velma tried to put on a happy face for her future lover.

"I know it's probably important for the study and all, but I'm concerned about all the weight I've gained. My right arm has been asleep for so long it's beginning to turn black. That placenta Lefty feeds me is so fattening! I do love it so, but if I was allowed to get up and walk around, I don't think I could do it. I've tried to tell Lefty he feeds me too much, but he ignores me and comes in the night while I'm asleep to fill up my hopper."

"It's his job, Peaches, and he's not allowed to vary the amount he feeds you." His smile was bigger and brighter than ever and then he left the room.

Velma weighed over a thousand pounds by the time Simon returned.

"Just exactly what is placenta, Doctor?"

"Why, it's afterbirth, of course. It comes out of the mother when a baby is born. Isn't that beautiful?"

Velma thrilled to see adoration in his eye. She wondered if he was dreaming of having a baby with her.

"Are there a lot of babies being born here?"

"No, no—none born here." His warm chuckle echoed hollowly within the metal contraption on his face. "The afterbirth is imported from all over the world, and the guys at our refinery puree it so you don't even have to chew."

Velma smiled, and then so did Simon. But this time the doctor's expression didn't quite work. His mask of affection slipped for just a moment and she caught a glimpse of his cold insect gaze.

With intuition's cold slap, all the fears she had been pushing down came rushing to the surface. But strangely calm, Velma asked the undeniable question. "This isn't really a study, is it?"

"Thank you Velma," the doctor said, the warmth suddenly gone from his voice. "That was getting harder and harder to maintain."

Velma pushed her rising panic back down. "But why—why are you forcing me to eat so much afterbirth?"

"Somebody's got to, and there are precious few women willing to do the job."

His voice was now absolutely lifeless. She missed his warmth. Real or not, it was all she'd had.

"Mothers are meant to take care of their own," he continued, "consuming it directly after the birthing process. It wouldn't do to have that stuff just lying around all over the planet. We tried tricking women into eating it, but that program has largely failed—too much of the stuff ended up on cigarette butts, cheeks, napkins, and the like."

"But why me?" Tears welled up from the dark holes containing her eyes. "I've never even had any children."

"Because you'll eat it," he said flatly, "that's why."

As he turned to leave the room, the voice in his mouth changed its tone again, uttering the word, "Sorry." Simon clapped his hand over the cage and quickly passed from sight.

Velma lay on her slab lapping up her tears for over an hour after Simon left her. "How did I get myself into such a mess? Oh Velma, you are such an ignorant, foolish woman. How could you be so easily charmed?"

Her sobbing subsided as she thought of the Doctor and his betrayal.

"He won't get away with it! As soon as I'm free of this trap, I'll teach him all about Peaches. I'll pull the cage off his mouth and let that poor fellow out. I'll beat the smug look right off his face. Then I'll find his legs, wherever they are, and snap them like kindling."

As big as she was, she felt she could do it. "He'd better not come too close," she said, swinging her massive left arm like club, "or he's had it!"

Her tears dried up and she licked at the last few as they trickled along the sweaty crease between her cheek and nose. She had forgotten just how tasty she was; and realized that just as she had never found food as satisfying as the stuff of her body, she found the products of other human bodies inferior in flavor to that of her own.

She had always indulged in a bit of Velma when she needed consoling, and as soon as the tears were gone, she missed them. If only she had more. Some of her own placenta would be nice too. She knew she couldn't have that, but she could have a bit of that blackened arm. Considering the withered almost crispy looking hand at the end of it, She was fairly certain she wouldn't feel a thing. Trouble was, she was so full all the time, there just wasn't room in her belly.

Something squirmed in her vagina.

A rat, a snake! What is it doing?

Velma panicked, bruising and lacerating herself as she quaked within her steel trap. Then she stopped fighting as another possibility occurred to her. "Are you about to have a baby, Velma?"

She felt it crawl out from between her legs. Straining to turn her head and get a look, all she could see were her massive mammaries. The thing seemed to be rolling as it moved along the crease between her left leg and mountainous belly. It rolled up her left side, along the back of her arm until, still unseen, it came to rest on her neck beside her ear. She felt a little kiss on her earlobe.

"Open your mouth wide," came a tiny voice with a certain fizziness to it.

"Who—?"

"Open your mouth wide and I will travel down your throat, slip myself over the end of the tube running into your stomach, and clamp down on it, stopping the flow of placenta."

"But why?"

"To help you escape, of course. If I stop the flow, you'll lose weight and be able to slip right out of your bonds. You saved me once and now I would return the favor. Hurry up, before someone comes."

"Gilbert? But what . . . I mean—"

Velma saw a flash of green and pink as it pushed its way into her mouth. She gagged on the little thing, then swallowed.

Would it do any good to panic? she wondered. Gilbert must have crawled inside me when Doctor Simon knocked me out in his office. How long ago was that?

Well, whatever he's been up to, Gilbert hasn't hurt me, and he thinks he owes me. Could be worse.

In considering her escape, she realized that Gilbert's idea of losing weight would probably do her no good. The metal straps which had expanded as she grew would surely contract as she shrank.

Velma could think of only one way, and Gilbert's efforts would not be wasted—she would need to have room in her belly. She tried to relax and wait patiently. With no windows and the low level of illumination within the facility remaining the same at all hours, it was difficult to gauge the passage of time.

Eventually, however, she did become hungry.

"It all began with boogers," she told herself, finally realizing the significance of the thought.

Velma began her escape by devouring her dead right arm. She had never consumed an entire body part before and relished every bit of it, finding it so damned delicious in fact, she couldn't stop and started in on her left arm.

The physical pain she felt could not compete in her brain with the anger she felt toward Doctor Simon. Within her head she pasted a smirk over Simon's impassive features, then imagined his pain and frustration when he found her gone. She was going to get out of here! The scrawny mad doctor would not have his way.

Velma heard the door squeak open as Lefty came in. "Hungrier than usual, I see," he said when he saw both Velma's arms were missing. The grotesquely disfigured man hopped over and checked her hopper. "Still full—must've been through here earlier in my rounds. Guess I'll see you in the morning."

Once he was gone, she did her best to wriggle free. She was able to get her head under the strap across her upper chest, but then her breasts were in the way. She removed them with her teeth and tried again. Still she was held tight.

Velma chewed her way through the next several hours and would have bled to death if it weren't for the rusted, dust laden mechanisms that dashed out of the walls to tie off her gushing blood vessels and cauterize her raw and oozing flesh.

She was a mess, but didn't care. All she could think of was the cold look on Simon's face and how he had tricked her.

Though she devoured her internal organs, the nasty little machines kept her going, splicing blood vessels and nerves into mechanical viscera.

When she bit into her stomach, she heard a tiny squeal and the small green and pink creature shot out and bounced away across the room, disappearing from sight.

As Velma chewed through her hips, her legs tumbled free and fell to the floor. She was in shock, blind to what she had done. All that was left intact was her head. Velma knew she would die, accepted it as her only escape.

Then she heard the door squeak open. Light streamed in and so did Doctor Simon. He casually appraised her condition.

"We'll rebuild you," he said. "We were going to do that anyway. A mouth that works like a wood chipper, a throat like a garbage disposal, and a stomach on wheels. We'll give you a powerful diesel engine so we can drive you anywhere in the five territories."

Oh no you won't, Velma thought.

As her lower jaw slid up over the top of her head blocking her vision, Simon's tone changed one last time, the desperate voice crying out, "Do it, Peaches!" Velma heard a tiny, but horrible scream just as she swallowed and disappeared.

PART II

A HERESY OF CORNDOGS

OPACITY AND THE DEATH EDITOR

with Eric M. Witchey

Coriander peered through the storefront's distorted window glass at a sign advertising Super Hard Man Spray and Perfect Eye Remover.

She wished she had some of that. So many johns weren't hard, and maybe if her eyes weren't so perfect the men would just fuck her and leave her. Perfect emerald Asian eyes bumped her price, but some johns were so smitten they became stalkers, and one had killed her.

Coriander's mother, a temple prostitute, was philosophical about death. She'd often said, "The woman who can do without the self-expression curious will shine through all eternity." It was an old saying, she claimed, and Cori figured Mom knew what she was talking about since she'd been dead herself for the last thirty years of her career.

Sometimes, Coriander wondered how long she'd need to be dead before the wise old sayings of the afterlife would start making sense. It made no sense to her that Koreans were the translators of choice for the afterlife. No matter what language the dead had used in life, official afterlife signs all appeared to them in their native tongue, and always mangled by Korean translators. She just couldn't fathom what Osiris, the Death Editor, saw in their strange twisting of earthly grammar. And, she had to wonder, what did dead Koreans see when they looked at afterlife verbiage?

She turned away from the window, strutted to her favorite curb, took another shot of fresh grave juice from the flask in her tiny, sequined purse, assumed her most seductive pose, and hoped a fleshy or a demon would take her up on her unspoken offer.

Two nights before, her first trick had been an angel—Zoriel or Zorkinel or some such thing. She'd finally given up on his name and taken to calling him Z-john. He was a smooth talker at first, saying how the brilliance of her soul brought him in like a lighthouse on a storm-tossed sea. She should have known better. Silver tongue in the morning, hooker take warning. He turned out to be the worst. He couldn't perform and he wouldn't shut up about himself and all the crap he had to deal with.

Even when she was alive—especially when she was alive—she figured the whole stand in line at the gates of Heaven shtick was pretty screwy. Being dead and meeting a few angels had cured her completely of any romantic visions of post-flesh eternal perfection.

So much for angels being guardians and guiding lights and such.

She'd been so depressed after listening to Z-john's self-pitying complaints for an hour that she'd broken out her happy whip and tuned in to the celestial choir on her ear bud. She'd whipped herself until the choir's song of peace became just flat harmony. Then she felt better.

Tonight, she wanted a little boost. A warm fleshy would be just the thing. Something about giving a living body ghostly pleasure was like going to hell but leaving the fun on. To ward off Z-john and his ilk, she turned out the lining of her formfitting sketch-webby so the Soul'd Out sign flashed on her delicately sculpted left shoulder.

The first drive-by was a bust. A fleshy, pre-teen called out, "Give me a year, babe, and I'll make your happy hair story."

Stupid kids, Coriander thought, flirting with loveless sex

even though they know it'll permanently disfigure their hearts.

A deep vibration in her concrete curb dematerialized her feet for a second before she pulled them together again. Then, a roaring, rattling cacophony echoed through the canyon of buildings. Just as she figured out which direction to look, a golden Egyptian chariot pulled by a huge, ebony war horse careened around the corner.

Earlene, a fleshy goth lezzy medium who walked both the wild side and the weird side often enough to have taught Coriander a couple new things in their first sessions, gave the leather reins a hard, practiced slap against demon horse ass. Army booted, black leather and lace BDSM babe that she was, the glitz chariot wasn't really Earlene's kind of ride, so Cori figured something was wrong.

A full-on skidding Ben Hur turn and slide stopped the ride broadside to Coriander, who renewed her effort to put all the spirit she had into displaying her wares.

A sign, now visible on the side of the chariot, said: "P.R. Inc.—Possessions and RePosessions—When you know you need something special, I am you."

Coriander strutted up to the afterlife ride. She said, "You don't need to go all Old Testament Cecil B. DeMill to get a date with me."

Earlene pulled in a couple gasping breaths before she managed to say, "It's not mine." Her eyes searched the street nervously.

"It's pretty cool for a live, white chick." All heat and promise, now, Cori licked her Cherry Promise red lips while tracing a hand over the lettering on the side of the war wagon. "What's with the branding?"

"I don't need a date, Cori. I need help."

Coriander's hope collapsed a bit. "You do know I'm working, right?"

"It's Opacity. My little girl was taken by a jackal-headed dude. I chased him down the alley behind Flaming Pete's. Almost caught him, too, but he just lifted up out of this ride into the sky, Opacity clinging for dear life to his neck and one hairy arm."

Opacity wasn't quite a little girl. She'd recently turned fifteen. Cori first met her when she was seven, and they had hit it off so well that Opacity once said, "When I grow up and die, I want to be just like you." It melted Cori's ethereal heart so completely that she'd taken to acting like a complete ass around Opacity, hoping the girl would turn to nobler aspirations.

Lately, there'd been signs of hope. Opacity had dedicated her energies to creating artwork good enough to sell to tourists through a street vendor. Just last week, an L.A. gallery owner sought her out and offered to represent her.

Cori said, "Tell me what happened."

Earlene shook a folded piece of papyrus in her fist. "I found this in the chariot."

Coriander took the scrap, opened it, and read the Engrish printed inside: Warn: The child forbids playing here, take care dangerously.

Cori might have been dead, but kidnapping an innocent fleshy pup still pushed all her female ass-kicking gauges into the red. That it was Opacity pegged her into deathly overdrive. "You say it was a jackal-headed dude? Was he all white kilty thing and black muscles like a Nubian shill at the Las Vegas Luxor?"

"You know him?"

"Anubis. Where was she when the dog-faced puke bagged her?"

"The alley behind my place."

"Between your apartment and the HIV clinic?"

"She hangs there and draws, you know? She likes to capture paper urine trousers and litter bags. Says it's real."

"Kid's got an eye. Her work captures the dignity of even the poorest of the poor."

"Can you do anything? I mean, I know I'm a medium and

all, but the guy was from your side of the veil. This sign," she pointed to the side of the chariot, "it's the same as the card left in my mouth after the last exorcism I performed. Remember the Mayan woman that died a few days ago, the psychic surgeon?"

Cori nodded. "Card in your mouth?"

"The possessing demon's calling card. You know, final message from the outcast soul?"

"Not part of my path, I guess," Cori said. "Do you still have the card?"

"It didn't make any sense, so I tossed it. On the back in subtitled hieroglyphs it said, You are my, is why I take you. Was it a warning? Is this revenge for helping the surgeon? Is it my fault she's gone?" Earlene, normally tough and sharp as cuticle scissors, shook from trying to repress an attack of sobs.

"I don't know what the message means, but I know something about the Jackal." Cori climbed up and took the reins.

"I can drive," Earlene said, "I was just getting the hang of this."

Cori slapped the horse's ass with the reins, and the black war horse faded to a transparent outline of itself, reared a little, and mounted the wind like one of Santa's eight dragging a chariot. "Rules of the dead." she said. "It can't fly for a fleshy."

The first pink of dawn streaked eastern clouds as the dark streets and exhaust-grimed buildings fell away below them. Earlene cowered below the fender, looking up at Coriander from terrified eyes. She opened her mouth to speak, but the wind snatched most of her words away, leaving only a few to reach Cori's ears. "The civilization is visited while lasting hygiene is thrown out." Coriander knew it was just the Death Editor dicking with the life-death interface again. She also knew, but wouldn't tell Earlene, that Anubis had the Editor's ear.

In spite of the corrupt interface, Earlene's words carried fear that distorted the wind wake behind them. Ignoring the sounds, Cori looked over her shoulder to read the eddies and whorls. Earlene was asking about the message: Warn: The child forbids playing here, take care dangerously.

Cori called out over the roar of physical and ethereal winds. "It means, The world of the living is too forbidding a place for the child and I will protect her from its dangers."

"Protect her? He kidnapped her!"

"Anubis is a hungry death god. For thousands of years, he has taken girls he believes are too pure of heart and mind for this dirty world." Coriander could sympathize with that— Opacity was too good for this world. But Anubis' remedy was worse by far. "He saves them from life and makes them his servants in the afterlife. She'll never grow older, but she'll essentially be his slave for eternity."

Earlene's heart-piercing scream needed no translation. If there's one thing the dead can hear, it's grief. Even a whisper of grief came to Cori's ear as a horrid, ragged, gut-tearing scream. She often wondered if this peculiarity of the afterlife was about the newly dead being drawn toward those who missed and loved them.

Luckily, fleshies can't hold an emotion long, and Earlene, sweet thing that she was, couldn't keep up her keening. It gave way to fearful whimpers which eventually subsided. Finally, she climbed to her knees, fierce determination burning in her eyes, and said, "Where is the pedophile?"

Cori had heard Anubis did indeed violate the girls he took. But she'd also heard he couldn't take any who weren't willing to go with him. "Almost there, Sweetie," she said.

"Where?"

"A graveyard, of course."

"Outside town? The St. Mary's Cemetery?"

"Valley of the Kings."

"Washington D.C.?"

"Egypt."

"That's on the other side of the effing planet."

"Honey, we're in a chariot pulled by a fiery-eyed horse

from Egyptian hell. We're already there, but we have to catch up with the idea of it."

"Cori?"

"Yeah, Babe?"

"Thanks."

Cori smiled and said, "Can't hear you. We're landing."

The sun set in the West as the chariot bucked and skidded to a halt. Sand and dust billowed up around them. Some of it passed through Cori, which gave her the kind of chill she used to get from seeing a tinted window roll down to reveal the vacant, cold eyes of some soulless perv who had money and no conscience.

She checked on Earlene, who stood and dusted off her leather bodice and black lace skirt. The woman's moon-silvered cleavage and shining blood-red lips made Cori regret the events of the evening. Things could have been so much more fun, so much more. . . .

Earlene looked up from her dust-off. Wind, sand, and dust had scoured the fleshy's face raw.

Cori's rising regret and desire dissolved into a vivid memory of the pain of living in the flesh. Earlene's face must hurt, but she showed no sign of her pain. Cori realized in that moment that her fleshy lover was willing to go to any lengths to save Opacity.

She refocused her ethereal attentions on their dark quest to save an innocent from enslavement.

Of the seven gates to the underworld, Cori only knew the location of one, the one through which she'd returned to the earthly realm after her judgment. Hidden behind the disabled-access toilet in the restroom of a touristy Egyptian souvenir vender, it led into a passage that ran to the underworld marsh beneath the Valley of the Kings. From there, it funneled into the Hall of Truth, where Coriander knew Anubis would have to pause for Opacity's judgment by the Death Editor—a.k.a., Osiris.

They abandoned the chariot, and Cori led Earlene into the antiseptic tile and chrome foyer of the underworld.

"An Egyptian wheelchair toilet? Really?" Earlene asked.

Realizing Earlene's fleshy eyes couldn't see the entrance, Cori took Earlene's hand.

The medium's gasp told Cori her ethereal touch had allowed Earlene to see both the sign posted over the commode and the entrance to the nether-realms. The sign said, Everywhere the pee without cave and spit, shit.

More Engrish.

Earlene said, "It doesn't make sense."

"It means don't spit, pee, or shit in the underworld, and you'd better pay attention to it. Bodily waste and fluids of the living are dangerously volatile in the realm of the dead."

"You're kidding."

"Do you need to go before we enter?"

Earlene winced a little, probably from the pain of her sandblasted skin. She shook her head. "I'm fine."

Still holding hands, they squeezed behind the sweating porcelain throne. In the passageway beyond, swirling blue, pink, and purple iridescence made rough-hewn, stone walls looked like massage oil spilled on wet, dark skin on a sunny day.

Earlene gasped and tugged back on Cori's hand.

Cori gripped tighter. "Don't pull. We have to keep touching. Don't let go, or you can't go back."

"I'm scared," Earlene said. "This is—"

"Not Kansas?"

"Not normal." Earlene's fingernails bit into the back of Cori's hand. The joys of being dead in the world of fleshies included walking through walls, going invisible, and other generally ghostly things. The drawbacks of being dead on the wrong side of the gates included being solid enough to feel pain as keenly as any living fleshy.

Cori said, "Jeeze, Babe, take it easy on the hand, there."

"You can feel that?" Earlene sounded amazed.

"You thought I couldn't feel it when we were together?"

"No. I mean, yes. I mean, I knew you could, but you always seemed so—"

"Ethereal? Beyond pain?"

"If I'd known it hurt, I would never have—"

"Did I ever use my safe word?"

"No, but—"

"Babe, we're in the afterlife. Here, the dead can suffer. Big time."

"But, I'm not dead."

"Don't let go of my hand for any reason or you get to stay, and you will most certainly get to suffer. Big time and for all time."

"What about Opacity?"

"Different rules. She's an innocent with Anubis." Cori pulled Earlene's hand to her heart. With her other arm, she pulled her friend into a tight hug. "It's okay, Babe. We'll get her out. Somehow."

Earlene pressed her face to Cori's neck. Warm tears pooled in the hollow of Cori's collarbone. "I'm sorry," she said. "I thought I was stronger than this."

"You took a flying chariot from an underworld god and chased after Opacity."

"But this. This is too fucking real. It smells like dead stuff and burned toast."

"It's not a happy place. If you're lucky, happy comes after your weigh-in." She pushed Earlene back and looked into her face. "Babe, you're the strongest fleshy I know. Most would be brain-muddled or on the ground bawling now. You have no idea how strong you are. You're upright, clear-headed, and on the scent—pardon the pun."

Earlene smiled and wiped at her smeared mascara, which made her eyes look sunken and dark. "I am a medium." She squared her shoulders and said, "Let's go."

Cori gripped Earlene's hand and led on.

Though time on the dead side wasn't the same, it only seemed like a few minutes before the reek of dead fish made them cover their noses. A few minutes later, their tunnel opened into a vast, round, water-filled chamber crowded with mounds of marsh muck and stands of papyrus sedge.

Their tunnel, like six others, entered from one hemisphere of the room like rays of a sunrise converging at the horizon. Centered in the opposite hemisphere, a single, white-walled tunnel exited the room. Carved hieroglyphs, sharp, new, and brightly painted, decorated the blocks of the arch. Bright light poured from the white tunnel.

Earlene pointed to a black, block-lettered sign over the white arch. "Another stupid sign?"

Like most souls who hadn't spent their lives talking to the dead, when Coriander was first hauled into the underworld, she hadn't been clear-headed enough to read the black, block-letter sign over the arch. She half expected "Abandon Hope all Ye Who Enter," but she found, Meets the soft love in the snow white world, bring dependence with instantaneous eternal. She shook her head and read it again. It still made no sense. "No effing clue, Earlene. Not one."

"Do you know where we are? I mean, there are eight tunnels here. Which one did they go in? Hell, are we even sure they went in any of them? It's a dog-headed god, and this is the afterlife, and what if she eats something or they make her drink blood or—"

"We didn't enter the afterlife from Greece. Neither did they."

"What the hell does that have to do with it?"

"Greek myth is where if you eat stuff you can't come back. Persephone. Whatever the path taken to the Hall of Truth, Osiris will pull out your heart and drop it on a balance scale. If it's heavier than a feather, they feed you to a crocodile."

As if to prove Cori's point, a spine-chewing, hair-graying scream rolled up the white corridor, spilled into the marshy chamber, echoed, then died in a wet, gasping gurgle.

Earlene screamed, "Opacity!" She tried to run for the white tunnel, but Coriander jerked her back, knocking them both off their feet onto a squishy hummock covered in papyrus. Through the fall and during the struggle to untangle themselves from the reeds, Cori kept her hold on Earlene's hand.

Finally, sitting beside one another, Cori said, "Earlene, you have to keep a level head or they'll be weighing your heart." She held up their clasped hands.

"We do this together. We have to smoke and make loud confused noises, or you and Opacity are both lost." She pulled out a pack of smokes and shook two up from the pack.

"What?"

Coriander grinned and said, "The smoke and loud noise will keep us hidden while approaching the Hall of Truth." She pointed the cigarettes at the white tunnel. "The Devourer of Souls, the croc I told you about, he lives here. Do what I say and we'll slip right past him. You have to trust me."

Earlene nodded. They lit up. Earlene, a living nonsmoker, coughed.

"Good," Cori said. "Add some whooping and hollering, splash your feet in the marsh water, whatever it takes to make a racket."

"Cori?"

Cigarette dangling from her lips, Cori blew smoke, stomped her feet on the grass, and moved into the stinky marsh water. She yelled around her cigarette. "What?"

"If you splash around in the water, I'm pretty sure it attracts crocodiles. I mean, it's a wounded prey sound."

"Honey, what's the opposite of alive?" Cori splashed into the water and pulled Earlene in after her.

"Dead?"

"Exactly," Cori said, fairly sure Earlene didn't understand, but equally sure her fleshy lover would feel the rightness of the splashing, yelling, and smoking. She was, after all, a medium, and, Cori knew from experience, the real deal.

"Oh!" Earlene yelled. "It's like calling the spirits but the other way around!"

"That's my girl!"

Splashing through muck and knee-deep water, they entered the white corridor and headed toward a distant bright light.

The bright light.

Twice, something under the water's surface pushed a speedboat-sized wake past them.

The first time, Earlene froze.

Two golden crocodile eyes the size of baseballs surfaced. Before their predatory swivel locked onto Earlene, Cori yanked hard to remind her of the underworld croc avoidance rules. Together, they screamed, smoked, and splashed.

The eyes submerged, and the wake moved on.

The second time, Earlene had the hang of the screaming and dancing, and the croc wake never even slowed.

At the end of their swampy tromp, they stepped up onto the first of seven white marble steps. A culvert through the center of the bottom steps let water move in and out of the corridor. The bright light came from an arch on top of the stairs. On each side of the arch, a ten foot tall Egyptian warrior statue holding a long spear guarded the portal.

"Okay," Cori said, "you can toss the cig, but don't insult anyone here."

As the cigs hissed in the water, the croc wake appeared from the culvert and pushed back along the corridor.

Once the croc was gone, Earlene looked around then asked, "Who would I insult?"

In unison, the two statues stepped forward. The stairs shook.

"Pale and Grim," Cori said.

"You're dead," the one on the left said.

"Pale?" Cori asked.

"No," the other one said. "I'm Pale."

"Sorry," she said. "You're identical."

"He's Grim, and you can tell the difference if you bother to try. Come on. Just because you're dead doesn't mean you need to be insensitive. The spears cross over the portal. Pay attention. Show that you at least try to care."

"I don't get it," Earlene said.

Pale frowned, "He's a lefty. I'm a righty."

Cori bowed.

Earlene followed suit.

When they straightened, Cori said, "I'm sorry. I've only met you once before."

"As if that's an excuse," Pale said.

Grim lowered his spear tip. "Can I poke them?"

"Not yet," Pale said.

"Soon?"

"I'll let you know."

Cori stepped up another step. "Look, guys, we've got a little problem, here."

"We?" Pale asked. "You're already dead. You shouldn't be here at all."

"I know, but we have to—"

Pale went on as if Coriander hadn't spoken, "She's not dead, so she shouldn't be here at all."

"Can I poke the fleshy?"

"Not yet."

Grim looked at his feet, obviously saddened by delayed gratification.

"Anubis took Opacity," Earlene said. "She doesn't deserve it. She didn't do anything wrong."

Pale lowered the point of his spear until it hovered a few inches from Cori's chest. "You brought a fleshy here."

"I had to."

"It's not her fault," Earlene said. "I made her. Anubis—"

The point of the spear slipped smoothly to the side until

it hovered just in front of Earlene's throat. "There are rules," Pale said. "You broke them."

Grim perked up. "Now?"

"Soon."

"I'm responsible," Cori said. "Give it to me."

"No," Earlene said. "Don't hurt her. It's my fault."

Cori pressed her fingernails into Earlene's flesh. "I know what I'm doing."

Pale pulled his spear back and chuckled. Coming from his white stone face, it sounded more like an avalanche than a laugh. "I doubt it," he said. "Being dead doesn't make you an afterlife lawyer."

Cori stepped closer to the stone bookends. "What would you know about lawyers? You're five thousand years from your last civilized debate."

"We have internet," Pale said.

"I like Hulu," Grim said. "I like Warehouse 13. We have friends there."

"Let me handle this," Pale said.

"Then I can poke them?"

"Probably."

"Okay."

"I broke the rules," Cori said. "You guard the threshold. You have to test me. Give me the riddle."

"Fleshy, here, confessed. She says she broke the rules."

"Now?" Grim asked.

In unison, Cori, Pale, and Earlene said, "Not yet!"

Poor Grim stepped back, his shoulders rolled in, and his head slumped.

"I'm sorry, Grim," Earlene said. "Opacity is important to me, and Anubis took her."

Grim looked up, and, Cori thought, even smiled in as much as stone lips would let him. "Thanks," Grim said. "It's okay. Everybody yells at me."

"Can we get on with this?" Cori asked.

"The fleshy claims culpability," Pale said. "The fleshy answers."

"No! You can't do—"

The point of Pale's spear against the hollow of Cori's throat stopped the words in her windpipe.

Earlene said, "It's okay. I'm good with riddles."

Pale pulled the spear a couple inches back from Cori's neck and said, "Do we have an understanding, Coriander?"

Terrified for Earlene, Cori nodded. "You told him you made me do this. You're a medium, so it's possible that you might have made me do this. Now, you have to answer a riddle if you want to enter the presence of the Death Editor."

"Your riddle," Pale said, "is as follows. When toothbrush is telephone it's as good as hairless milk."

"What?" Earlene said.

Cold, stone eyes on Cori, Pale repeated, "When toothbrush is telephone it's as good as hairless milk."

"That's no riddle," Earlene said. "Riddles are questions. What happened to the sphinx thing?"

"Greek, again," Cori said.

"The sphinx is Egyptian."

Pale said, "The sphinx let too many people in. That's why we're here."

Grim nodded.

"Riddles are still questions," Earlene said. "What's the question?"

"That's part of the riddle," Pale said.

"Foul," Cori said. "It's not a test if she can't understand the riddle. It's Engrish. You have to let me translate."

"You'll spoil it." Grim said. Stone dust rained down from his frustrated, furrowed brow. "It's too easy if you translate. I'm poking them." Grim's spearhead came down toward Earlene.

"If you kill her," Cori said. "what happens next?"

Pale pushed Grim's spear aside. "She'll stand before Osiris."

"Oh," Grim said. "He's got a thing about rules."

"And?" Coriander asked.

Quietly, Grimm said, "Riddles have to be questions."

Coriander put her hand on her hips and took on her mother's scolding tone. "What's wrong with you guys? Have you gotten bored in the last few centuries? Does the Death Editor know you're giving folks a hard time just for fun? You want to lose your jobs?"

Pale said, "Okay, you broke rules, we broke rules. We're even. We all agree to keep it quiet, and we'll let you answer the riddle."

Coriander smiled, nodded, and said, "Snake oil."

Pale said, "You cheated."

Coriander said, "I'm right, aren't I?"

Grim's shoulders sagged so precipitously, a crack formed at his left armpit. He and Pale stepped aside to let the women pass.

"How'd you get that?" Earlene asked.

"Ask me later." Cori moved past Grim, avoiding the falling dust.

"Cori?" Earlene tugged her back.

Earlene was looking up into Grim's sad, stone face. "Isn't there something we can do for them? I mean, we sort of tricked them, and all."

Grim's huge, stone head moved slowly from side to side. He said, "It's okay. It happens. I go whole eons without poking anyone."

Pale added, "Fair is fair. You were right. We were just being nasty. Try standing at a threshold for six thousand years or so and see if you don't try to spice up your death a little."

Cori said. "I kinda enjoyed it."

"Really?" Pale asked.

"Me, too," Earlene said. "I'd have been disappointed if it were the same old riddles I heard in grade school."

Grim was still looking, well, pretty grim.

Earlene went on. "Grim, if it will make you feel any better, you can poke me a little. Not too hard, though. I'm a fleshy."

Grim's shoulders straightened. He lifted his spearhead from the stairs. "Really? You'd do that?"

"Earlene," Cori said, "Opacity's going to be weighed."

"They're pretty backed up," Pale said. "War in the middle east, famine in Africa. A tsunami in Malaysia. It'll be a while before their number's called."

Earlene said. "My safe word's 'grotto.'"

"Huh?" Grim said.

Pale shook his head. "I'll show you a web site later. For now, if she says 'grotto,' you stop."

"Grotto," Grim said. "Yeah." He moved the point of his spear close to the bottom edge of Earlene's goth corset. "Here?"

She nodded. "You're a big boy. Not too hard, now"

Grim pushed the point of the spear into the corset.

Cori winced.

Earlene giggled. "That tickles."

Grim beamed. "That's fun. She laughed. See, Pale? She laughed."

Earlene said. "You can push a little harder if you want."

"Let me try," Pale said.

"They always scream and beg," Grim said.

Pale said, "You're the first to laugh. Let me!"

"Opacity," Cori tugged on Earlene's hand.

"Please? One poke?"

Earlene nodded.

Pale poked with amazing care for a ten foot tall stone man.

She giggled her pleasure and gasped for breath.

The two grinning giants stepped back, bowed, stood straight, touched spearheads at the top of the archway, then said in unison, "Coriander and Earlene, who have entered the afterlife with selfless purpose and bested us, the guardians of the gate, pass into illumination and judgment. May your hearts be light."

Cori and Earlene stepped under the spears. As they passed under, Grim whispered, "Come back and play again."

Pale added, "Please?"

Earlene winked and said, "I like you guys."

Cori dragged Earlene quickly through the arch and down the seven steps on the other side.

The chamber was an inside-out pyramid. The four brilliant white walls rose smoothly to a point high above them. A sun-like sphere hovered at the apex of the pyramid, the source of light at the end of the tunnel. The floor, also made of brilliant white marble, could have been home to several World Cup games at once had it not been for concentric squares made of straight rows of marble benches surrounding the circular dais at the room's center, right where you'd put a razor blade if you wanted to sharpen it.

An aisle ran between each row of benches. From three corners of the room, a larger aisle led through the rows of benches up to the dais.

The stairs entered where the fourth aisle would have been had it not been for a canal running from the culvert under the stairs all the way to the dais. There, murky water filled a round swimming pool about the right size for a Southern California bungalow back yard.

At the very center of the dais, the afterlife light hovering above him, Osiris sat in a straight-backed stone throne capped with a soccer ball-sized gold disk set into a pair of stylized wings. Decked out in clichéd Walk-Like-an-Egyptian clothing and jewelry, he looked more bored than deific.

People sat waiting on every bench in the hall. All of them looked drugged, dazed, and confused. A few wandered in the aisles like lost Alzheimer's patients.

Some wore torn and charred military fatigues. Some wore robes or sarongs or blue jeans and T-shirts. They came in all shapes, sizes, and races. Turbans told her some were Sikhs. Ya-makas marked some as Jews. She spied a nun in full, black habit as well as monks in saffron.

"They're from all over the place," Earlene said.

"Every person has a path," Cori said. "Every path leads here."

"To Egyptian judgement?"

"Everyone sees a different metaphor for spiritual growth."

"I'm Wiccan. I don't see Hecate or Inanna."

"We came in the way I went out. It's Egyptian."

"Those guys up front," Earlene said. "What are they writing?"

On the shortest benches nearest the center, four to a bench, brown-skinned, shirtless men and women bent over rolled papyrus, styluses in hands. From time to time, one of them looked up, spoke to Osiris, then returned to his or her work.

"Translators," Cori said. "There's a lot of language work, here. They're kind of like court reporters and translators rolled into one. They make sure the dead understand Osiris, and they make sure he understands the dead." She scanned the chamber. "Do you see Opacity?"

"No. Are you sure she's here?"

"Unless she's already been—"

A feminine voice that sounded suspiciously like the voice that did every airport page Cori had ever heard echoed through the room. "Now serving number seven million, eight-hundred ninety-thousand three-hundred twenty-two. Now serving number seven million, eight-hundred ninety-thousand three-hundred twenty-two. Please proceed to the dais for weighing." The message repeated in a number of other languages until a man in a dark silk suit stood up, checked the ticket in his hand, then walked down an aisle toward the dais.

"Seven million?" Earlene said.

"Who knows when they started counting?"

"I suppose."

"Look for Anubis. A dog-faced god should be easy to spot."

"Maybe we should get a number," Earlene said.

"Yeah. Good idea. If we can't find them, we'll still want to talk to Osiris. He'll know where they went."

Earlene pointed, "There. On the wall. What's that sign mean?"

Cori read the sign. You number may to serve healthy flesh breakfast the information hall of meat move on.

Below the sign hung a red plastic number dispenser just like the one Cori had used at the DMV before she died. "Good eye, Love."

They hurried to take a number, all the time searching for Anubis and Opacity.

As Cori pulled their number from the dispenser, a gong sounded from the dais. She and Earlene looked toward the source.

The silk-suited man, now kneeling before Osiris, screamed, "No!" He managed a "Pl," too, before Osiris pointed an ankh at him and the man flew through the air like a tossed doll. He splashed down in the pool before he got to the "ease" part of his plea. He surfaced, screamed and swam for the edge.

The boat wake of the croc appeared in the canal, moving at racing speed toward the swimming pool.

The wake splashed over the man's head and shoulders. Water churned. When the water calmed, the suited man was gone.

"Oh my god," Earlene said. "The croc got him?"

"Oh, yeah," Cori said. "Big time and forever."

"We have to—"

The airport voice said, "Now serving number seven-million, eight-hundred ninety-thousand three-hundred twenty-three. Now serving number seven-million, eight-hundred ninety-thousand three-hundred twenty-three. Please proceed to the dais for weighing."

ALAN M. CLARK

Across the aisle to Cori's left, Anubis stood. He was holding Opacity's hand, and she looked as stuporous as any soul in
the room.

Coriander pointed, then she quickly brought her hand
back to cover Earlene's mouth and stifle the shout about to
leap from her friend. "No," she whispered into Earlene's ear.
"You're alive. They don't like that here."

Earlene nodded.

Cori pulled her hand away.

"Is she dead?" Earlene asked.

"Pedo-puppy's consorts have to be death virgins."

Earlene took a deep breath, swallowed hard, and asked,
"What do we do?"

"We try to cut them off before they reach the dais."

Hand-in-hand, they threaded their way between benches
and down a corner aisle on a collision course with Anubis.

Coriander figured the snatching part might go pretty well,
but she didn't really have a plan for the run-away part after-
ward. If things deteriorated into a fight, they couldn't possibly
win.

"If she's alive, how can they weigh her heart?" Earlene
asked.

Without thinking, Coriander said, "Anubis can pull it
out."

Earlene froze, pulling Cori to a dead stop. Tears streamed
down Earlene's face.

Coriander realized her mistake and tried to make up for it.
"He can put it back, too, with no harm to her. It's part of his
shtick."

Earlene blinked back her terror, and Coriander checked
Anubis' progress.

They'd hesitated just long enough to let jackal-headed Anubis and vacant-eyed Opacity beat them onto the dais to stand
before Osiris.

Contempt oozed from Osiris' godly voice. "So soon? They

last forever, but your desire does not."

Ignoring Osiris, Anubis grasped Opacity's shoulder with one hand, set the long, clawed fingers of his other into the shape of a spearhead, and cocked his arm over Opacity's chest.

Earlene struggled to rush forward, but Coriander brought her up short again.

The commotion caught the attention of the gods.

Anubis turned hungry, yellow eyes toward them. A snarling growl slipped past his fangs and under his curling lip.

Coriander stepped forward, trying to use her body to hide her friend.

"Great Osiris," Cori called out. "Among the living, there is a name for what Anubis does with young girls."

A scribe on a bench near the dais spoke, "Among the living, there Anubis is the name for a little girl does he with the name."

"Words of the living have no power here," Anubis said.

The scribe said, "Living fight no words on premises."

"The great and fair Osiris values a light heart. Will you allow Anubis to place a darkness and weight in this girl's heart?"

The scribe said, "You, the value of illuminated woman blood muscle to place night stone in to allow Anubis."

"Why is he repeating what you said, but getting it wrong?" Earlene whispered.

"Everybody hears their own language."

"It's English, but it's like the signs."

"Engrish. Osiris likes bad Korean translations. I don't know what to tell you. Maybe it lets him judge more objectively."

"Weird," Earlene said.

Anubis growled in a dead tongue Coriander couldn't understand.

A different scribe responded. "Who this progress to impeding? Your death blood muscle scaled long ago."

Cori said, "I am one of many who love this child, who has only just begun to live."

The scribe said, "I no degrees love this child one of who starts to live soonest now."

Osiris spoke rapidly in the same language as Anubis, adding a dismissive gesture.

A different scribe translated. "I allow your intrusion, Coriander, because I remember you fondly. It is worthy that you try to save the girl, but Anubis has this right."

"My pale, dom ass, he does!" Earlene surged forward, dragging Cori up onto the dais. "You dog-faced son of a bitch, she's only fifteen. You fucking let her go or I'll neuter you right here, right now!"

In less than one of Earlene's heartbeats, a thousand thoughts spun into and out of Coriander's mind. Things had gone from pretty bad to desperately oh-my-gawd fucked up in seconds. She had really wanted to avoid the full attention of two gods in the afterlife.

In spite of her struggle to anchor the medium to the floor, Cori ended up facing off with Osiris, Anubis, and Opacity. Earlene's spitting, hissing rant continued. Tiny droplets of saliva flew from her lips and exploded like firecrackers tossed on the marble of the dais.

Osiris lifted his ankh, and Cori decided she had to do something now. Words worthy of her mother came from her mouth, "Birth mother of meat, one picks must have some livings!" While surprised scribes and gods turned their full attention toward her, she stopped pulling and instead pushed closer to Earlene, putting her lover off balance. Just as Earlene was about to fall into the lap of Osiris, Cori set her feet and yanked back, spinning Earlene in place and pulling her into a bear hug she hoped the fine fleshy couldn't break.

A translator looked up at her. He narrowed his dark, almond-shaped eyes in concentration.

"Translate it," she said.

The translator spoke, "Born of a mother, flesh should have a choice in life."

Osiris' bored eyes opened wider.

Anubis lifted his black bumpy jackal lip, revealing predatory canines. His low, nasty growl spoke more eloquently than the translators rendition of it. "Walker dead earth in to suffers also all in all of time."

Cori used her free hand to flip Anubis the afterlife's universal gesture of one-fingered contempt. To Osiris, she said, "Let's we are enjoying good lawmen times."

This time, the translator smiled at her. He seemed to be getting the hang of her ploy. He turned to Osiris and said, "Through all of time, we have valued honorable men of the law."

Osiris bowed his head slightly.

Anubis cocked his hand over Opacity's chest.

Earlene screamed, "No!" She hacked up a loogie, lunged, and spat. Perfectly aimed phlegm sailed through the air and exploded in Anubis's eye. While the jackal howled, Earlene broke free of Coriander, crossed the distance to Anubis, and slammed the hard toe of her leather army boot into the center of his very human maleness. The dog, god or no, folded up and slumped to the floor.

"Shit," Cori said.

The translator turned to her and cocked an eyebrow.

"No," Cori said.

He nodded.

Cori figured they were croc bait. Instinct told her to grab Earlene and Opacity then run like hell.

Lunging after her lover, she glanced at Osiris. In one of those freeze-time-in-crisis moments, the image of the god's contorted face burned itself into her memory, where it would, for all of time, struggle to suppress a grin.

Coriander got a grip on Opacity and Earlene, then backed them away from Anubis. The two heroines and one damsel in distress turned as one toward the exit aisle, which was barred by two giant stone men holding spears.

All three women stood helpless between the gasping Anubis, the not-quite-laughing Osiris, and the dangerously bored brothers Pale and Grim. Pale said, "You wait at the door for a thousand years, then in one day you get enough fun to last you for the next thousand."

Grim, whose cracks seemed to have healed up nicely, said, "Thanks." He looked at Osiris and said, "Who do I get to poke?"

Pale nodded to Coriander. "Sorry," he said. "Nothing personal. It's the job, you know?"

Osiris, god of honor, judgment, love, and resurrection, stood.

The Jackal recovered from his booting enough to growl, though he didn't quite manage the low register he had earlier.

Osiris' voice filled the pyramid so completely it drowned out all other sounds, including echoes. "Be still in my presence or suffer."

The translator said, "Not to move—"

"Oh, shut up," Osiris said.

Swallowing his next word, the translator bowed his head.

Anubis apparently decided he wanted a turn contributing to the mayhem, and he leaped for Opacity.

But the ankh is quicker than the eye. At the top of his leap, he hit an invisible wall and fell to the floor.

"You," Osiris said. "Sit! Stay!"

Anubis sat.

"Oh shit," Earlene said.

Opacity said, "Earlene?"

"That's right, Baby. I'm here."

"I like this movie," Opacity said.

Cori focused on the surprising, uncertain, and potentially horrible attention of Osiris. She bowed deeply and said, "Oh, honored one who saw fit to spare me once from the jaws of suffering and final death, thank you for your lenience."

"Coriander," Osiris said. "I knew you were trouble when

your heart weighed dead even with the feather."

A light cloud of pale stone dust wafted over Cori's shoulder. She suspected Grim, or maybe Pale, was stifling a laugh, but she didn't dare turn to look. "I apologize most humbly, Lord of the scales. I am here now on behalf of another in a matter of honor. May I speak?"

"Honor?"

Coriander felt the weight of his eyes on her chest.

"You," he said, "come from a long line of priestesses. Speak of your knowing of hearts and of flesh. But I warn you, Coriander who walks in two worlds, as you stand before me, three hearts balance against the weight of a single feather and the words you now give life."

Coriander went down on one knee, bowed her head, and said, "Lord Osiris, I alone am responsible for bringing this living woman into your domain. I did this for love of her and the living child Anubis has stolen."

Osiris caught the eye of the errant translator and said, "Grass pies a boy cow making."

The translator said, "Bullshit."

"It's my fault," Earlene said. "I made her do it. This asshole took Opacity. He rolled up—"

Grim's spear interrupted, pushing on Earlene's corset and sending her into a spasm of giggles. "Stop," she managed between gasping and guffaws. "Please." She fell to her knees. Both Grim and Pale worked her over with their spear tips.

Osiris waited patiently until, nearly out of breath, she said, "Grotto!"

Grim and Pale backed off, apparently satisfied with their work.

"Well," Osiris said. "That was different."

Cori said, "Anubis brought Opacity through the Egyptian gate, but she doesn't know this place, you, or Anubis."

"All paths converge here," Osiris said."All hearts know their own truth. The scales are just."

"But weighing the heart of a child makes the heart of a mother heavy."

"The child is not an orphan?" Osiris' eyes darkened and he looked down on Anubis.

"Earlene isn't exactly her mother," Cori said, "but she's the closest thing Opacity has."

Cori went on. "Earlene found Opacity on the streets, alone, without a clue about how to survive. She was seven, then. Earlene has raised her the best she could. I've helped as much as a dead hooker can."

Osiris said, "Your words might sway living hearts."

Desperate, Cori looked around. On every bench of the chamber, suddenly clear-eyed men and women watched the judgment of the three women. Behind her, stone-faced Grim and Pale also watched.

Anubis sat and stayed.

Earlene had gotten up from the floor, folded her knees beneath her, folded her hands in her lap, and closed her eyes. Her regular, slow breathing told Coriander the woman sought the guidance of spirits. She'd be no help at all.

Opacity clung to Earlene's shoulders.

Worst of all, two crocodilian eyes watched from the nearby swimming pool of doom.

It was all up to her. If she could seduce angels, then maybe, just maybe, she could give Earlene and Opacity a chance. "Honor, then," Cori stood, taking on the power of her life and afterlife, the wise teachings of her mother, and the traditions of a professional lineage stretching through the ages to a time before the birth of even Osiris, a time when knowledge of flesh and spirit hadn't been separated one from the other by thought. Coriander gathered to her the light and wiles of trade and flesh and spirit, and she became the light of desire in the presence of Osiris.

A collective gasp hissed through the ranks of onlookers. The sound of cracking stone came from behind her where Grim and Pale stood.

Anubis whimpered, a pathetic sound that would have melted her heart had it not come from a dog-faced pedophile.

Coriander strode forward toward the god of honor and judgment. "What honor is there, My Lord, for any of us, flesh or spirit, if we don't honor actions born of love, be they a woman's embrace of a lost child or her defense of that child in the face of insurmountable odds?" She took another step toward the god. Deep in her belly, she willed the spark of lust to flare and rise to light her eyes and words. "I stand before you, all-seeing Osiris, and await your will. As are we all in the end, I am yours to do with as you please." She lifted a hand to the dark skin of the royal chin and traced a finger from ear lobe to lips.

Osiris' dark eyes held hers, and she felt the thrill of knowing she had him and would know him in ways he would gladly pay for, and the price would be the freedom of her friends.

But he laughed. "Isis would flay us both for the rest of eternity," he said. "Still, it is truly amazing that you wield a knowing so ancient that not even I remain unmoved."

Her freshly kindled flames died, and Coriander, ancient seductress, became once more just Cori the ghost in trouble. "Shit."

"As I said, I am moved. However, I am also bound by this office."

Cori had no idea what to say, what to do. Grab and run was out. Earlene was fetal in some goth medium attempt to make contact with the afterlife, which was of course where she was. If she were lucky, she might make contact with the living, but that wouldn't do them any good. The dog man was licking his lips and making sad puppy eyes at Opacity, and Opacity knelt beside useless Earlene, head on the older woman's shoulder like a little girl trying to fall asleep in her mother's embrace, except she was looking at Anubis like he was her puppy and any second she'd go scoop him up and hug him.

"I got nothing," Cori said.

"No," a gravelly voice said behind her. She turned.

Grim, spear in one hand and the other hand on his marble hip was shaking his head. "No," he repeated. "I won't have the best day of my eternity end with you giving up. You break into the afterlife hauling a fleshy with you to save an innocent from eternal goings-on I can't even imagine, you beat the croc, you challenge my brother and me to a game of riddles and win, you get the knack of the puzzle-lingue to catch the attention of an eternally bored god, your friend puts the hurt on the Jackal, which I have to tell you was the highlight of my day, and now you're going to give up? No. I don't think so."

"Grim?" Cori stared at the previously monosyllabic, poke-obsessed stone guardian.

"What?" the brother Grim said, "You think because I get the job of being all obsessed with poking people that I can't think for myself and put a few words together?"

Beside his brother, Pale's smile cracked his lips and pushed fissures across his cheeks. "You tell 'em, brother."

"I have a certain investment, here," Grim said. "And you, Coriander, are going to make it pay off. You get your feces co-agulated and fight to get your buddies out of here. If you don't, I'm telling you right now that I will be the one who pokes you and tosses your sorry ghost hooker ass into the pool."

Stunned, Cori stared at the suddenly articulate stone guardian. "Uh, okay," she managed. Still not sure what to say or do, she turned back to Osiris. "Okay," she said. "What have I got? The dog pulls up his silly Possession and Repossession chariot."

"His what?" Osiris asked.

Anubis spoke quickly from his seat across the Dais. "I pretend to run a business. We all need a cover to move freely among the living."

Osiris nodded his assent.

"So," Cori continued, "he pulls up in the alley where Opacity draws pictures. He grabs her—"

Anubis stood. "She grabbed me!"

The ankh moved. Anubis' teeth clapped together and he fell back to a sitting position. "Go on," Osiris said.

"Then," Cori said, "Earlene catches him, and he bolts. She takes the chariot and comes to me for help. We come here." She needed a triumphant close, but all thoughts, feelings, and memories were riding a spin cycle in her heart. "Honor?" she said. "Innocence? Art? Love? Family? Too many religions? I don't know."

Osiris said, "Then time to talk is over." He lifted his ankh.

"Art!" Cori yelled.

Anubis' hand paused.

"How about this?" she said.

The ankh went back down.

Anubis shook himself like a dog fresh from fetching a stick in a pond. Then, he said, "She asked to come."

At that, Earlene popped out of her trance. In unison, she and Cori said, "What?"

"The Jackal cannot take a child who is unwilling," Osiris said.

Opacity stood from Earlene's side. Her eyes were somewhat clearer, but as she spoke, her voice was lifeless and monotone. "He was going to take you, Mom."

"Me?"

"You killed the psychic healer," Anubis said.

"Liar!" Earlene snorted up a new loogie and lunged for the dog-face.

All at once, Cori yelled, Opacity screamed, Pale and Grim pushed forward to stop the collision of jackal god and fleshy fluids, and the ankh rose and fell.

Silence echoed throughout the chamber, and everyone, Cori, Earlene, Opacity, Anubis, Pale, and Grim found themselves sitting and staying.

The croc eyes blinked, and a long snout appeared on the surface. Cori could have sworn it was smiling.

"You," Osiris pointed the ankh at Opacity. "Explain."

"Mom's a medium," she said thickly. "This old lady Mayan psychic surgeon was possessed. Her daughter paid Mom to do the exorcism."

"Possessed by me," Anubis said.

"He admits it," Earlene said.

"Psychic surgeons," Anubis said, "have to be possessed to do their operations."

To Opacity, Osiris said, "Go on." His tone made it clear that the next person not named Opacity who spoke would hurt a lot.

"Mom expelled Anubis, but she didn't know he was going to help the old lady do open heart surgery on herself."

"Because he can remove a heart and put it back," Osiris said.

Anubis' long snout bobbed up and down in emphatic agreement.

"So," Opacity said, "the old lady died. He was after Mom because she interfered."

"The debt was owed," Anubis said.

Osiris nodded.

"The girl," said Anubis, "offered herself to save her mother."

"How did you know he was going to take me?" Earlene asked Opacity.

"I was drawing in the alley and I blacked out like you do when you're in a trance. When I woke up, I saw I'd drawn a bunch of pictures all about the dog-man taking you to hell. Then he came looking for you and I offered myself in your place."

"Honey, you've never shown anything like that kind of story-in-picture ability before." Earlene pulled Opacity close and hugged her.

It suddenly struck Cori that she'd had the old dog wrong all along. He'd been trying to heal hearts as best he could. So had Earlene. Everyone was giving up someone for someone else, and all because the selfish, shortsightedness of a psychic surgeon's daughter had set them all against one another.

Nobody was wrong, here. Everybody was right. And Cori found that she suddenly hoped the ghost of a not-so-wise hooker could counter balance the lives and loves of mothers, and daughters.

A new voice entered the conversation, a high, almost bell-like voice. "I'd like to add something."

Cori knew the voice. "Not now," she said. Fucking angels were the worst.

Zorkiel, or Zorial, or whatever the hell his name was, descended, wings wide, from the bright light at the apex of the chamber.

Normally, he looked kind of gray and his wings drooped behind him like they belonged to a dead pigeon who was following him around. Now, his face beamed and his white wings glowed, and his golden halo shone so brightly that Cori had to hold a hand up to cover her eyes. In fact, Cori thought, his head and wings looked a lot like the sun and wings on Osiris' throne.

The angel touched down between Coriander and Earlene. "Ta-da! I'm here, Honey," he said.

"This is really bad timing," Cori said. "I'm not working."

The angel laughed, and the sound of bells filled the chamber. "Earlene called me. Divine intervention, Love. It's my job. Guiding light and all."

Earlene looked disgusted. "Took you long enough."

Osiris propped his elbow on the armrest and his royal chin in his royal hand. "Interesting," he said. "But you know they came in through the Egyptian gate, right?"

The angel said, "And you know it doesn't matter which gate they come in. In the end they're all going to the same place."

"You're only supposed to manifest for people who use the third gate."

"Whatever," the angel said. "My girlfriend, here," he gestured toward Coriander, "has walked the path of a thousand paths, and you know it."

Osiris nodded. "Ancient wisdom," he said.

"You're different," Cori said. "What have you done to your wings and halo? Even your voice."

"Flesh and spirit are one," Zorial said. "The dog god is no villain. The little girl is hope and heroism."

"Uh, yeah?" Cori said. "And you're all light and happiness now."

"You know it, Coriander," the angel said."

Confused, Cori shook her head, then looked at the translator, hoping he'd shed some light on what the angel said. The translator just grinned.

Pale said, "Congratulations, Coriander!"

"For what?"

"The annihilation of dualism," Zorial said. "You figured it out."

"Oh, that," Cori said, grateful to the previously hated angel and certain it was best to pretend she had figured it, whatever it was, out.

"That explains her balanced scales," Osiris said.

"And you know how this has to go, now, don't you?" Zorial said. "The little girl has talent that can teach understanding."

Cori saw a chance while the angel and Osiris debated the rules and regs of the afterlife. She crawled over to Earlene and Opacity.

"We have to get out of here. Now." Cori pulled on Earlene's hand, but her hand passed right through Earlene's.

"What the hell?" Earlene said.

Pale said, "The fleshy broke contact. She's a shade, now."

"How do I get her home?" Cori asked.

"I don't know," Pale said.

"Osiris can do it," Grim said.

"I'm not going if Mom can't go," Opacity said.

126

Coriander jumped up and pushed past Zorkling's feathery wings. "Guys, can I say something?"

"I'm trying to get you out of here," Angel Z said.

"Really?" Osiris said. To the translators, he said, "Take a break, boys."

The translators apparently didn't know what to do with a break, so they put their pens down, sat quietly, and watched the afterlife circus unfolding before them.

"I'm responsible for this," Cori said. "And him." She pointed to Anubis, who was clearly very unhappy about still sitting and staying.

"We're all listening," Osiris said, "and waiting."

Pale and Grim, in unison, said, "Give 'em hell, girl."

"Uh," Cori began, unsure if what she had to say was worth anything on the scale of hearts. "You guys all have believers among the living, each religion setting its own agenda when it comes to sin and redemption."

"Not just among the living," Osiris said.

"Fine. But in the end, here you are, Osiris, a god of only one ancient religion, among many religions, but you weigh the hearts at the confluence of all religions."

"You see what you expect to see. I hold this position because I am known by many names and by all of them I am just and incorruptible."

"And how did you achieve that reputation?"

"I perform my duties with integrity."

Yes, integrity. That's it! Cori thought.

"Integrity is a matter of the heart, yours as well as those who stand before you to be judged. Sins committed by the owners of each heart are determined by the individual's beliefs. If one feels one has sinned, it weighs heavily on the heart."

"Sin is a matter of willful violation of personal integrity." Osiris sounded like he'd had this conversation many times over the millennia. "One might learn a lesson from making a sinful choice. A heartfelt lesson then reflected in deed lessens the weight added by a sin. However, when one continually violates personal integrity—"

"Yes, but my point is that since a good heart is determined by the individual in a subjective manner, the living are afforded a certain power over their own lives. Free will. The ability to choose and to learn."

"Yes."

"Opacity is too young to make the choice of standing in for her mother. Anubis should not be allowed to take her."

Osiris said, "She was on hand and saw an opportunity to help her mother. Opacity made the choice. Life includes chance. Without it, choices would be meaningless. Each manifestation of godhead creates both mayhem and good fortune among the living. Both are distributed purely at random. We cannot use these powers to manipulate the living. I manage dementia and miscommunication."

"You also manage rationality and clarity in justice."

Osiris nodded.

"One side without the other is meaningless," Coriander said. "They define each other. In a sense, they are the same thing."

"I told you she got it," Angel Z said.

"And Anubis?" Cori asked.

"Grief, possession, healing, and hope."

"So," Cori said, "in his case, possessions can be mayhem, as in demonic possessions, or beneficent, as in helping a psychic healer. That covers the 'Possessions' part of the sign on his chariot,'P.R. Inc.—Possessions and RePosessions—When you know you need something special, I am you?' So what's the 'RePossessions' part mean?"

"A bit of flair," Anubis put in a little too swiftly "A clever turn of phrase is all."

Earlene spoke up. "Yeah. The same ad was on the card in my mouth after the exorcism on the psychic surgeon. On the back, he wrote, 'You are my, is why I take you.'"

Osiris' eyes narrowed as he turned toward Anubis.

The jackal said. "Merely coincidence. A note I lost. I wrote it on a card because I had nothing else," His nervous eyes avoided Osiris' face.

"You told me it was written in hieroglyphics, in which case it made no sense," Cori said. "But translated from Engrish—"

The grinning translator finished for her. "You take what is mine; I take what is yours."

"You took the heart he was healing," Osiris said.

"So he took the heart you were healing," Cori said. Suddenly, Cori felt bad for the old dog. She felt bad for the psychic surgeon even though she'd never met the old woman. Most of all, she felt bad for Earlene because of the way the scale was, or rather wasn't, tipping.

But Earlene's eyes grew wide with realization. "You were never going to take me. You knew you were going to take Opacity the moment I cast you out of the old lady or you wouldn't have left the note on your card."

"I see what you mean," Cori said. "She wasn't taken at random. She was taken as revenge."

Osiris sat up straight, his eyes still on the jackal. "Again?" his voice boomed and his eyes burned so brightly the predator gaze of the other god withered.

Osiris lifted the ankh, and Coriander closed her eyes and ducked.

In the big god voice that filled the chamber, Osiris said, "Get up, Jackal."

Cori opened one eye to peek.

Anubis stood straighter than Pale and Grim. He whimpered a little.

"Is this true?" Osiris demanded. "Did you take the girl as revenge?"

Under the honor-binding gaze of Osiris, the jackal's neck muscles strained as if he were trying to shake his head. However, his long, black muzzle moved up and down instead and then his mouth opened and, as if against his will, a confession tumbled out. "I possessed the girl and made her draw the story of her mother's fate."

"Preying upon the noble sympathies of an innocent is a serious breach," Osiris said. "You have reached a new low."

He turned to the women. "You can go. All of you."

Cori opened her other eye.

Angelic cheers rang in her ears. Avalanches of joyful laughter rolled over her from Pale and Grim, and stone dust swirled around her so thick she could barely see the ten feet to the edge of the pool where baseball-sized eyes shed crocodile tears.

Coriander blinked and wiped her eyes, and when she could see again, it was the dawn of a new day, and she stood on her favorite street corner with Earlene and Opacity at her side.

Z stood in the street glowing and grinning. "You are amazing," he said. "I'm going to send the other angels your way, and I wouldn't be too surprised if you start seeing a few of the others dropping in on you."

Confused and not yet truly sure they were all safe, Cori asked, "The others?"

"The Mayans, the Egyptians, the Buddhists. You know, the guys from the eight paths to the afterlife."

"So we're really home?" Cori said. "Earlene? Are you—"

Earlene pinched herself and yelped. "Flesh. I'm okay, Cori. I'm just fine." She threw her arms around the neck of her ghostly lover and planted a warm wet one on her.

When Cori managed to untangle Earlene from her neck, she asked Z, "I don't get it. They let us go, just like that?"

"Anubis screwed up. Revenge is not a manifestation of chance. And, I think it didn't hurt that Osiris kind of likes you. Not many people balance the scales perfectly."

"What's that got to do with it?"

"Your mother did it. You did it, and I'd be willing to bet that Opacity will do it, too."

Earlene said, "You said he whined all the time. I think he's kind of nice."

"I whined because Cori hated whining," Angel Z said. "Guiding light and all that. When her heart opened enough to see Anubis as more than just a pedophile dog, she also saw me as more than just a whining john. She can see all the facets of the universe without assuming one excludes the other."

"Annihilation of dualism," Opacity said.

"Exactly," Z said. "Anubis is me. I'm him. We're Osiris. You're us. We all just invent the differences."

Cori still wasn't sure she understood, but she liked that Z's little speechifying had made Opacity smile. What she did get from it was that maybe Anubis was still running around loose. "Am I going to have to deal with the dog again?" she asked.

"Do you hate him?" Z asked.

Cori looked at her friends then searched her heart and found that it was lighter than a feather. "No," she said.

Z winked, spread his wings, and lifted off into the heavens.

"I'll be damned," Cori said.

"I kind of doubt it," Opacity said.

"I'm going to take Opacity home," Earlene said. Arm protectively around the smiling teen, Earlene started to turn to leave.

"Earlene?"

"Yeah, Babe?"

"Amorous this place twice us."

"I love you, too, Cori."

MAMA'S MAW AND THE PAWS

with Bruce Holland Rogers

One afternoon, I'm in my neighbor's backyard when he's not home, burying a beloved kitten that died of a bad temper, when it hits me. (Not the kitten, but an idea. It did have its claws out though. Not the kitten, but the idea. The kitten was dead.) Mom is widowed and retired. She's eccentric. Her hatred of cats notwithstanding, she'd make a good old cat lady. If she sold the house and moved in with me and the cats, I could train her! Even though Mister Mac has told me Mom is still dangerous, I know she can't be as dangerous as she was when I was a kid, and that had all worked out. I have most of my teeth, for instance, and my bones have all healed except the head bone. In fact, all those years down in the Thinking Hole have mellowed Mom, whether Mister Mac admits it or not. She has killed hardly anyone in years, and her most recent shenanigans have been kind of routine, the sort of thing you can see coming and avoid if you sleep with one eye open and a hammer under your pillow. It's like she can't think of any real good killings after drowning her colleagues in chocolate sauce, so she doesn't try so hard now.

I don't know what it is about her, but I can't help myself. She's not pretty, but she is somehow very attractive. Six husbands, although they are all dead now, does say something. All right, I say to myself. Mom's moving in.

Convincing her to sell the house will be easy. It has grown dry and flakey and so cumbersome that if I give her the slightest nudge, she'll shed it in one piece like last year's skin. Besides, with new digs come new rules and she's got to know that at my place she'll be out of the Thinking Hole for good, no matter what Mister Mac says. The tricky part is convincing her to love what she really hates. How am I going to do that? I decide to go to my favorite place, the library, for answers. Like most readers, I don't really enjoy the books as much as the information I get from them. They seem to know this and don't cough up that information readily. I don't mean most readers. They cough up stuff easily if you slap them on the back, especially while they're eating or smoking. But the books, they're the ones that don't give up their information easily. I spend hours researching something and get virtually nowhere.

If you want something from books, you've got to dress like you mean business, so I put on the coat of writhing woolies, the boots of wilting, and my library gloves. The librarian can tell right away I have come for information. As soon as I step through the doors, she says, "You look like you mean business!" But then she shakes her head. "It's too bad you didn't come yesterday." What can she mean? Why does it matter what day I come to the library? Then I hear the sounds of muffled moans. The moans of books, that is. I look over at the rows of shelves, and I see the top of a tall black hat moving among them. I catch the smell of machine oil and hear the rattle of locks and chains. What is Mister Mac doing in the library?

"I wouldn't, if I were you," says the librarian. "He's lost his keys again." But asking Mister Mac is maybe even better than asking the books. I go among the shelves. Mister Mac, with loops and loops of chains and locks wrapped around his neck and hanging from his arms, is holding a book in one hand. In the other, he holds a bucket of bad weather. He's just been dipping the book into it, and the pages are wet and cloudy. He frowns when he sees me. "And what do you know about it!" he says, and pitches the bucket of bad weather in my face.

I should have seen it coming. He's done it before. This time it contains a hail of brown beans and what feels like shredded fiber glass insulation against my bare skin, but is probably just a heavy sleet. Lightning singes my nostril hairs. Every batch is a little different, if only because Mister Mac wants to make sure that folks don't have the opportunity to dress properly. But how does one dress for beans?

"Innocent!" I say, which is always the first word a person should say when meeting Mister Mac. "Wasn't me!" And now that I have testified myself safe, I brush off the beans and say, "What are you investigating?"

Then I notice the Bag of Inquisition there on the floor by his feet.

The bag is moving, and Mister Mac picks it up and pulls out this man I've never seen before. His face is all swollen and purple on account of Mister Mac having been Inquisitive with him, so I give the fellow a sly wink and say, "Oh, guilty of bruising! Into the Hole with him for a hundred years!" But the man just closes his eyes and groans, and I guess the poor fellow has all but kicked the humor habit.

"He's been teaching cats things they shouldn't know," says Mister Mac.

"Such as?" I ask.

"How to win the hearts of dog people," he says. "Cats versus dogs has always been a polarizing issue. Without it politicians will be denied an important tool for manipulating the national discourse. Very subversive."

Mom has always preferred dog. "The feline won't come to me—too independent, but I can work with the canine," I've heard her say, and I know she would rather stand in the doorway and shake a flaming dog than allow a cat into her home. I've seen her do it—a ghastly preparation for consuming the poor thing at the dinner table. She's always been good at manipulating a dog into jumping into her boiling pot. Still. . . .

"Mister Mac," I say, "do you remember how you helped Lord Peel to slender himself down?"

"On the Rack-of-No-Thank-You," says Mister Mac. "Yes, I remember."

"But before he turned himself in to be skinnied, he plumped himself up, didn't he? And why did he do that, Mister Mac?"

He doesn't answer my question. He's looking at the books behind me. "My keys," he says, "are somewhere. And one of these books knows where!" He raises his bucket. It is full of weather again.

"Lord Peel fattened himself up before the Rack, Mister Mac, so that in the end, if he lived, he could be twice as proud of all the fat he'd lost."

Mister Mac's eyes have gone all squinty. He shakes the bucket, spilling a few snowflakes and a gust of cold wind. "Keys," he growls to a thick leather-bound book. "What do you know about my keys?"

I say, "Why don't you give me that fellow in your sack, and I'll fix it so he can be twice as sorry for getting certain people to like cats."

Mister Mac is all about punishment, but he usually likes to be the one dishing it out. Even so, he's forgotten his keys for the moment and I've got his attention. The cold mist around his bucket has lifted a little and a slice of sunshine leaks out. It is the first time I have ever seen Mister Mac smile. It is a terrible thing and I shield my eyes and turn away. When I look again the smile is gone and I see a trio of tiny seagulls, glistening with crude, perched on the rim of his bucket where they could not possibly exist.

"And just how would you go about doing that?" he asks and the gulls do a little dance, stamping their webbed feet and fluttering their sodden wings, bespattering the titles of nearby books. "It wouldn't involve your wicked mum, would it?"

"Might be," I say. It wouldn't do to lie to him. "Some would count it a punishment to be sent to visit her. Maybe we shouldn't risk it, though. She might go too far, and then you'd have to deal with her."

Mister Mac shows his teeth. "You'd both go into the hole, if anything serious happened to the prisoner. I'm the only one allowed to get serious!" He picks up the bag and thrusts it at me. "Take him, then! But I'll be investigating afterwards!"

I sling the bag over my shoulder—it is surprisingly light—and hurry away. Behind me, I hear Mister Mac say, "Now, what was it? Something about the books . . ." I don't want to be in the library when he manages to remember that, once again, he has lost his keys. My tricycle is where I parked it. "Here we go," I tell it. I take a paper bird out of my pocket, then pat myself for matches. There aren't any! I pat myself again. How am I going to set fire to the bird?

I can hear Mister Mac's voice suddenly getting loud inside the library. Probably he is remembering his keys. There is going to be some very bad weather in there any moment now.

"Come on, come on," I say to myself. "There's not that much difference between burning and not!" I look at the sun, which is a fiery spot in the sky, and I hold the paper bird up so that the edge of its tail just covers the sun. "I worry that you don't burn," I tell the bird. "I worry about it just a little bit." I have to be sure not to worry too much. Too much concern, and it won't work. I fret. I stew. But I am careful not to obsess. Well, that does it. I finally manage to get the bird lit with some small concern and a trick of the light. I've worried just enough so that one wing starts to burn. I let go, and the flaming bird rises into the sky. "To my Mama!" I tell the bird. And to the tricycle I say, "Follow that bird!" The tricycle jumps forward. We are on our way.

I have completely forgotten that paper birds fly as the crow flies and that they don't make allowances for those following them. If you cannot keep up, you will lose your guide. I remember that this warning appears in 14 point bolded type on a fold-out section of the breast of each one. But like most consumers, I forget to reread all the instructions before consuming.

When the bird flies toward the sea, I know that Mom is sunning herself again among the Archipelago of Arch Enemies. And, of course, instead of keeping to the causeways, the bird cuts straight across the marsh and out to sea. It is too late to rescind the command to my vehicle—I will have to ride it out or lose my trusted contraption. The tricycle is an amphibious model and makes fairly light work of the marsh. But hitting the surf, pedaling fiercely, it is all I can do to keep my nose above the surface of the waves.

The gods, they say, live outside of time, but the itty-bitty god that lives in my waterproof wristwatch makes me painfully aware of the slow passage of time. I become exhausted as the day wears on into night, my face pruned up so tightly that I can barely keep my eyes open and I nearly lose sight of the paper bird. If I drift off numerous times into dreams of Mom and Mister Mac hugging, kissing, and eventually making passionate love to one another, I am unaware of it. I do not remember dreams. If I lose consciousness at all, I can't tell because the bird is within sight each time that I look up and wonder if I have been sleeping.

I'm afraid, though, that the bird will burn up before we get to Mom, and because I have let such a thought come into my head, that very thing happens. The paper bird is now just a scrap of ash drifting in the wind. I'm in a pickle now, because even though I have another paper bird in my pocket, I can't get it out without stopping my pedaling. If I stop my pedaling, the tricycle will sink. The sea is already reaching up with watery fingers now and then to throw salt on the handlebars and make them rust. If the trike starts to sink, there is no way that the sea will let it rise to the surface again.

"Mama!" I call out. "Mama, I am lost and forsaken! Call me home to your bosom, oh dear Mama of mine!" I feel embarrassed saying "bosom" about Mom, but it's part of the incantation. I see clouds on the horizon, and gray mists. I keep pedaling though I feel that my legs might fall off. I recite the incantation again. The mists get closer. Finally, I see them. My Mom's great bosoms are rising and falling like rough, gray goose flesh. The waves crash against them. I pedal like mad now for the safety of my Mom's bosom, but the sea senses that the tricycle might get away, and mechanical crabs rise up from the deep and try to climb aboard. One of them gets onto the front fork and starts to loosen a nut.

If it is true that the Eskimo have many different words for snow, then I suppose I should have a lot of different words for NIGHTMARE. "Why does everything in my life have to be so difficult?" I shout, kicking at the crab adjusting its crescent wrench claw. "I have never done anything to deserve this aggression from the sea. I don't think I have ever even urinated while swimming.

"And paper birds," I scream, as the ash finally settles on my flailing tongue, "you should burn LONGER. You should notice when the sea is giving your charge a hard time and slow your burning to account for it."

I try to spit it out but realize I've swallowed it. It tastes awful and that fuels my rant. But I am done with these petty concerns and I turn to the real source of my anger.

"Why do I have to return again and again to such a treacherous mom? How many times do I have to be battered and beaten against her perilous reef and wash up a wreck upon her shores? Why is my love for her renewed each time she patches me up?" Yes, I am angry with her, but I am also afraid. I have never before questioned the love of my Mom and I am grateful that her head remains submerged, her hearing compromised.

But the lowering tide exposes the causeway of her cheek. Her forehead emerges from the waves and then the delicate bridge of her nose supporting a lone traveler who looks just like me. She fixes me with one eye and I am afraid. I know I must say something. "Mister Mac should admit his passionate feelings for you, Mom!" I roar across the waves. "Who does he think he's fooling anyway?"

The traveler looks up, surprised. I see a stirring in Mom's bosom at my words and although I have suspected it for some time, I'm now certain that she has feelings for Mister Mac as well.

"Mom! I think everything could turn out fine in the end!" I shout. I have brought my tricycle closer and closer to where the waves are breaking. "Mom!" I shout. Something is swelling in my heart. Something is swelling in my heart. Oh, something is swelling in my heart, and I don't think it is a clot of blood. I think it is filial love. Maybe I have needed to tell my Mom it's okay to be whatever size she needed to be, whether smaller than a brine shrimp or bigger than some islands. Maybe I have needed to encourage her to reach out to the one who has loomed in her life like a penitentiary . . . the penitentiary of love! I'm not here because of cats. I'm here to speak to my Mom of the force that drives us all. Love! Love! The prepackaged purpose—the cats—was something I needed to arrive here. But now I see my true purpose. I am cupid, ferrying an arrow for Mister Mac across the briny sea.

I am happy! But the traveler on her nose, the man who looks just like me, has a stern look on his face. He folds his arms. He says something I can't make out, and something rises from the dripping folds of Mom's neck. It has three wheels, gleaming metal spikes, and black and red streamers on the ends of its handlebars. A BATTLE TRIKE. I'm pedaling as hard as I can, come ashore with a little bump on the margin of Mom's flesh, when the battle trike rings its little bell. It is a dolorous bell, a funereal bell, in spite of being so small.

Mom slowly opens her mouth and says one word. She says, "Un-son." And the man on her nose, the man who looks like me, he says something this time that I can hear. He says to the battle trike, "Sic 'em," and climbs on.

How stupid of me! Didn't I just admit that I chronically take her abuse and return to her only love and forgiveness each time? My selective memory makes it easier to love everything about her, even the very things that caused so much pain. But the truth is she understands the cycle better than I do. The more pain I am willing to endure, the more evident my love is to her when I ultimately forgive her.

Mister Mac doesn't love her. He loves that she deserves punishment.

She doesn't love Mister Mac. She loves his intense scrutiny of her crimes and the attention she receives when he judges her and hands down his punishment.

She's done imagining my internal struggles to love or hate her—she created the Un-son and his battle trike so she can actually see me battle it out with myself. But which am I, the son who loves her or the one who hates?

Somehow this question reminds me about Mister Mac's prisoner, tied up in the sack lashed to my trike's rear wheel platform. My fingers are numb with cold from my ocean crossing, and as I pick at the knot at the top of the sack, I do my best to explain the situation to him. I tell him that I know that he didn't choose this battle, but now he's in it up to his neck, and if he wants to escape with his life, he's going to have to figure out some way to help me. The battle trike and Un-son are cresting my Mom's bosom. It's downhill from there. They will be upon us soon. I bite the knot, loosen it. I tug, pull, pick at the knot. Finally, the bag falls away, and the man rises to his feet and blinks in the bright sun.

"Nye urd," he says. His face is swollen. "Nye urd." He's looking at Mom, and I realize he's trying to say, My word. "My word, is that the Bitch Goddess herself?"

"How do we fight this battle trike?" I say. I look at our own tricycle, which wobbles sadly on wheels loosened by mechanical crabs. I want to command it to advance and take up a defensive position before us, but it's so weak. "Easy, boy. Steady," I say. I try turning some of the loose nuts with my fingers, but metal is falling away in great flakes of rust.

"The Dog Catechism," says the man from the bag, the cat

lover. It's amazing that I can understand him. "Fight the cat-echism, not the trike. He has it, see? It's a questionnaire written on the dog he carries inside his shirt!" He is pointing, and it does look like there's something under Un-son's shirt, some-thing wriggly that might be a small dog.

I don't have much of a choice. All my attempts to reassure my trike fail. It begins to weep in heartbreaking sobs of its little toot horn. This is the end. It crumbles, and the next wave washes it into the sea. The wave after that erases all signs of my three-wheeled friend and companion. It's just the man and me standing on the sand as the battle trike hurtles toward us. "Say 'Avast!'" says the man. "Say, 'I choose trial by catechism.' It's the only way!"

Un-son's eyes are full of hate. For Mom? For me? I don't know which of us is which. Maybe Mom means that I am the Un-son and he is the true son. Does it matter? All I know is that his expression says we are enemies and one of us is doomed. I say, "Avast!"

Apparently that's all it takes. The Un-son hits the breaks and his trike grinds to a halt, leaving an angry welt on Mom's breast. He whips the dog out of his shirt and begins to read from its pale belly. It is strange hearing the words come to me in my own voice.

"Receiving as we do the grace of food, shelter and petting . . ." He pauses to part the fur to reveal an obscured portion of the text. ". . . what form of love do we provide our masters in return?"

"This is a question for a dog," I complain to the prisoner.

"Just answer the questions. I know them all. It's how I teach cats."

"But—"

"Cats don't have butts. Not like we do or say a horse has." He gets all dreamy-eyed and says, "A horse has a great ass." Then he seems to focus again. "Dogs have butts too and isn't that what we're dealing with here?" He gives me a disgusted look like he knows I'm stupid or something for not having thought about this before. Finally he says, "The answer is Un-conditional Love."

I provide the answer. The Un-son continues and the questioning goes on all day, the whine of little tiny motors, like artificial mosquitoes, making it nearly impossible to concentrate. I'm thinking this poor concentration is unreasonable since I'm not even the one having to come up with the answers when it strikes me. (I don't mean the Un-son. Not that he's not mean—he's mean all right—but he's still rambling on with his religious doggy doctrine.) What strikes me is the realization that the sound of those motors is coming from the Un-son. He is not another me after all. He's another mechanical device, not unlike the crabs that destroyed my trike.

"Look," I say, taking a step back toward the water. "Why don't we settle this with a wading contest?" If I can get him even ankle-deep in the water, maybe the crabs would go to work on him.

"You chose the catechism," says the Un-son. He insists we stick with my Mom's shaggy questionnaire.

"The whole point of my being here is that I want to talk to my Mom. Why can't I talk to her?"

He's combing through the dog's fur with his fingers, trying to read the next question. He frowns. Maybe some of what is written on the dog has faded. He puts the dog down. "You can't talk to her because she's molting," says the Un-son. You may have noticed that she's rapidly outgrowing her house. This is a dangerous time for you. He squints. "It's a dangerous time for all of us. I'd just as soon be clear of your mother, even if she did make me what I am today."

Mom's breast quivers uneasily beneath us and I know she doesn't like what he said.

But it all sounds familiar to me. It feels right. He speaks for me as well! What happened to his hostility? Could it be that the Un-son is only partly mechanical, the rest is very human and he has identified with me as well? Have I found a long-lost brother?

Today, I have encountered several mortal dangers, all of them pulmonary, but none of them physiological: I have loved and feared, hated and hoped! But most of all, I find I am confused and bewildered!

I face my twin. "I too am mechanical," I tell him, my eyes welling up with tears.

The prisoner pats me gently on the shoulder and reaches up with the soiled cuff of his shirt to wipe moisture from my cheek. This is a little weird, but I'm thinking he feels he owes me for saving him from Mister Mac.

"I react without thinking," I tell my robotic brother, "becoming a tool for those who know how to use me."

Mom's breast quakes and we are all three thrown off our feet and I know she likes what I have said even less. We slide down the slope of her breast and come to rest on the faux-wood siding of her house. The structure curves across her ribs, wraps up around her shoulders with epaulette-like gables and dormers and disappears beneath the waves to cover her submerged lower extremities. Mom's body grows too fast and loud cracking comes from the structure of her house as stored energy is released. The wall beneath me splits open and I see the studs inside, the sparking ends of broken wiring and ruptured plumbing. Mom has never molted so precipitately. As her chest swells and we rise high into the sky, the structure of her house comes apart, exploding around us. The prisoner is thrown free with a chunk of decorative belly-band. The last I see of him is the expression on his face. It is one of regret, perhaps an apology of sorts. He knows I will have to answer to Mister Mac for his loss.

My twin is reaching down to help me up. "I understand completely," he says. His embrace comes just in time to protect me from the explosion. Gas from a ruptured pipe must have found the sparking electrical wires. I am hurtling through space. My twin is no longer with me, but the dog is wrapped in my arms and licking at my face. I do not recognize the landscape that passes far below us.

With an embarrassing squelching sound and massive spray, we land in the lapping surf of a resort beach. Nearby sun bathers give me a disgusted look. Some of them move away chewing on resentment, mouthing words just beneath my threshold of hearing.

"Come on, pup," I say, gathering the dog in my arms as I stand. "We've got to get out of here!" I don't know how we're going to do that, but I want to get as far away as possible from Mom's molting. She's mad at me. She might or might not be molting with malice, but her eruptions are just as dangerous either way.

I'm thinking I should warn the sun bathers, but I don't like their attitude.

That's when I see the battle trike. I jump onto the platform over the rear wheels, settle the dog on the seat, and grip the handlebars. "To safety!" I cry. "Take us to safety!"

Which is how I end up back at the library, where Mister Mac casts the Net of Correction over me. I try not to move, because there are fishhooks woven into the net, but that doesn't do me much good since the next thing Mister Mac does is gather the net up like a bag. He slings us all over his shoulder—me, the dog, the battle trike. He takes us to the Thinking Hole.

I say, "What did I do wrong?"

Mister Mac says, "You tell me!"

And so begins my punishment in the Hole. These days it is an interstellar prison ship. I'm given the job of keeping the poop deck mucked out and walking the dogs as we head to Barnard's Star. Because there are a lot of rats onboard, ratters, mostly small terriers, are employed to keep their populations down. I thought there would be cat boxes to clean too, but the dogs' union has interstellar shipping sewn up. The cats' union has claimed maritime shipping.

My incarceration has lasted an entire two weeks and now we have returned to Earth. I'm informed that Mister Mac says I have done enough Thinking and I am being released. I am frustrated by this as I have made some canine friends and am just getting good at my job.

I pat my favorite ratter pup on the head and debark. Apparently this allows the creature one credit against the No Barking rule strictly enforced aboard ship and he uses it to bark his goodbye to me.

Now I realize my true punishment. One hundred years have passed here at home. In the spaceport, I pick up a newspaper and read about a new continent that has formed far out to sea. The new land is very attractive, perhaps unnaturally so, they say. It seems to call out to explorers from all across the globe, but their ships are smashed upon the rocky shores. The few survivors, sailors and the ships' ratters, are never heard from again, assumed destroyed or consumed by some unknown force. From far away, the continent is said to resemble a woman.

By now, the battle trike is in a museum. The dog has died of old age and is also in a museum, stuffed, displayed next to what is supposed to be a transcript of the catechism, but since no one is allowed to touch the fur and look directly at the marks on the preserved skin, who can say if this text is the true scripture? The dog doesn't look much like the one from which Un-Son read the questionnaire.

I do miss my Mom. I hire an airship to fly as close to her as the pilot will dare to get. For a continent, she is hard to find. This cloudy first day of our trip, the airship circles and circles. Mom doesn't seem to be where the charts say she should be. Then, very faintly, we catch the awful stink of death. Overnight, the airship corrects course, and on our second day, the outlines of her grisly shores hove into view.

"Mama, my mama," I cry. But of course she can't hear me. She is nothing but a rocky shore, and mountains, and jungle, and desert now. She is nothing but a place for ships to run aground.

As we move closer, we can see the remains of countless

mariners that litter her jungles and steppes, her arid and desolate plateaus and even her mountains. We fly into a valley where the more recently dead are revealed. My mother has destroyed them all. Their bones are picked clean.

I assume that she will destroy anything that comes ashore, but as we float up her right torso and arrive at her shoulder, we see innumerable tiny creatures devouring the rolling hills of her upper arm. The limb separates as we watch and begins drifting out to sea. I turn to view her head, once a gentle bluff, now a bald cliff face etched with anguish and pain.

We fly lower to get a better view of the ravenous creatures at her shoulder, and as we do it becomes clear that they have overrun her entire upper torso. Since the ships started wrecking against her, the surviving ratters have bred in incredible numbers. And they're unionized!

Mama once said, "The feline won't come to me, but I can work with the canine."

The landscape below is overrun with cats.

On impulse I excuse myself from the bridge, enter the bowels of the ship and cut open the gas bladders that hold us aloft. Within minutes the crew of this ship will be added to the castaways that litter the landscape below. I suspect I will not perish with the rest, as Mother no doubt has other plans for me.

MOUSENIGHT

with Jill Bauman

Winter was a difficult time for the community of blind mice known as the Rodenthall. Their whiskers, which they depended upon like a blind man's cane to help them get around, became worn out as the year progressed, making it difficult for them to get around and forage for food. Many went hungry. Some died of starvation or fatal injury. A few, unable to find their way home, wandered off into the wilderness, never to be seen again. Life was hard until that time when their feelers could be replaced. Through the cold wintry months they hibernated in the hundreds of tunnels riddling the ground of their homeland, each family claiming a separate tunnel as their own and emerging only when absolutely necessary.

Snuggling closely with her family to keep warm in the darkness of their burrow, Petey-pea tried to sleep time away. She knew that, with time, they would all gain new whiskers in an event as mysterious as life itself. With new whiskers life would become much easier again. If only she could sleep until then. And she would too if she didn't ache so terribly, and have to periodically join the rest of her family in leaving the burrow to forage for food.

Feeling a tongue licking the long gash in her thigh, Petey-pea awoke. She thought it was her mother; it smelled like her mother. The licking helped to clean the wound and make it feel better, but it did little good for the broken bone in Petey-pea's right forepaw, her perforated ear, torn snout, and broken ribs. Nonetheless, she made soft noises to acknowledge her mother's efforts.

With her powerful sense of smell, Petey-pea could distinguish each of her family members by the odor of the blood coming from the wounds they each had sustained while stumbling about outside over the last couple of months.

She heard a soft gurgling in her stomach and knew they would all be awakening in a few more days and filing out of the burrow in search of seeds and roots buried in the snow. Each time they went out they had to search farther and farther afield for food with whiskers which were progressively more frayed, split, and broken, thus increasing the chance for disasters.

Petey-pea tried to remember how it happened that they all got new whiskers each year, but couldn't seem to focus on the event. Her memory of the past month seemed clear, but beyond that it became increasingly cloudy. This was the way of memory, she knew, but it troubled her now to think that if only she knew how the whiskers came about she might find a way to achieve them sooner and end the suffering.

The whiskers she bore in her cheek sockets were worse than useless, having become a hindrance. Just last week one of the feelers which was bent in three places steered her wrong and she'd gone over an icy precipice. She'd fallen into a frozen bramble where a thorn opened the gash on her thigh. At the time Petey-pea didn't know where she was. If her family had not found her, she might not have made it back to the burrow.

When the whiskers betrayed her like that, she felt so horribly helpless. Sadly she plucked from her fuzzy snout what remained of her whiskers and dropped them to the dirt floor, then turned over and went back to sleep.

The community of blind mice awoke as one, as if by some unheard alarm in every burrow home, and they all knew the time had arrived. It may have been the smell that awoke them. Petey-pea could indeed smell the whiskers falling from the sky outside. Though she hadn't known it until now, this was what she had been waiting for; what they all had been waiting for. A tightness grew in Petey-pea's tiny chest, there was a surge of energy through her body, and she suddenly had to be outside. Nothing would stop her.

The rest of her family seemed to have found their feet at the same time she had, and squealing, they all rushed for the tunnel exit, creating a jam there at the opening. Petey-pea could feel the cold air from outside licking at her face. She had to get out.

Someone—it smelled like her sister, Galeta-pea—bit her on the shoulder. Feeling the blood running down her side, she broke free of the jam and stumbled forward on her hind legs with outstretched forepaws, feeling her way out into the open. Her heart leapt into her throat as she heard the insane squealing that filled the air, and felt the crazed horde of bodies surrounding her tugging at her insistently, wanting to bear her along with them. She swallowed hard as she joined the storm of blind mice, all rushing, shoving, pushing from their earthen homes and swarming for the hills. Throwing caution to the wind, she ran as swiftly as possible, willing to do whatever it took. There was only one goal—WHISKERS—sacred, and oh, so precious.

Petey-pea felt the sharp sting of the whiskers falling from the sky as they pelted her head and back, and she fell to all fours in the snow and began her search. Her right paw closed on a whisker, but just as she was about to thrust it into an empty, calloused socket in her downy snout, it was wrenched from her grasp, and she squealed angrily.

Kicked and shoved, elbowed and pummeled from all sides, Petey-pea quickly gathered up more of the sensitive black wonders which littered the ground, and one by one, drove them into her cheeks until all the sockets in her snout were filled. Now she was not so lost. She could easily feel her way around, and began the process of gathering spare whiskers which she would hoard through the coming year.

Clawing and biting, Petey-pea fought with those who came too close. She recognized many by their smells; members of her own family, mates with whom she might one day soon have a litter. She was heedless of the pain she caused them, heedless too of her own injuries.

Her forepaws were overloaded with whiskers when another Rodenthall bowled into her, intent on plundering her spoils. She fought the creature off, taking a furry chunk from his ear, but lost half her trove in the process.

Feeling around in the snow, she found the whiskers were all taken and so started for home with her burden. On the way she stumbled over the lifeless remains of those who had fallen in their struggle for the whiskers.

With the loss of a few lives there would be more for everyone. Those who made it to safety with their booty would live well for at least another year.

Petey-pea was the first of her family to reach the safety of their burrow home. She dug a hole in the tunnel wall in which to hide her treasure, dumped them in, and covered them up. She would return for the whiskers as she needed them to replace those which became worn out.

Although she had no understanding of numbers, she sensed that she had returned with too few of the feelers for the coming year. She might get by if she were careful with each and every one of them. If she had a litter within the next year, she certainly would not have enough.

Eventually her father and sisters, Galeta-pea and Voltina-pea, returned and secreted their booty in the burrow. Life had returned to normal, and now that they could feel their way around, there was lots to do.

Petey-pea's mother was not missed. The dead outside were forgotten, left to feed the carrion-eaters and melt away with the snow, as the mousy Rodenthall began their preparations for the new year.

PART III

BONE-GRUBBER'S GAMBLE

THE MUSTY COW'S TEAT OF DEATH

with Jeremy Robert Johnson

As cute as the dog was, I was going to slather and roast the creature and devour it with the help of my best friends while throwing whore's shoes in an outdoorsy, afternoony sort of setting. My neighbor, the pup's owner and master, a sweet fellow by the name of Ordwello, would be pissed.

But the social gods are fickle and demand offerings. I tried to appease my friends with a sack of rice, but it turns out I'd suffered an otic malfunction. Thus I was forced to proffer a blinding magnitude of blazing bunnies (which are a lot like kettle kittens and church dogs, but burn brighter and bluer). Even with this, I was threatened with a charge of Improper BBQ Etiquette, a crime that finds itself punished via the slickening sight of neighborly sickle-to-the-gut-coils. I was pre-unraveling inside my grey slop when I heard the familiar bark.

Of course! I'd burlapped Ordwello's pooch this morning when it attempted to landmine my lawn with noxious dog tootsie.

On presentation of the bagged canine my friends holstered their cursed sickles and the one filling out the citation put away his clipboard. They backed away as Ordwello burst through the fence to reclaim his pup, the cream inside his blue egg such a delicious odor it practically demanded a hatchet to the forehead.

But Neighbor Brains were a Sick-Maker, however delicious

and piquant, and I hadn't the proper BBQ outfit to keep his meat blocks leaking an hour of sticky stew. Bad prep was no prep at all, and that's per the long-running President of BBQ Trackademy. Ordwello should have let the dog go, and let peace fall upon all of us via greased esophagus. Instead he invaded by means of yard-wounding fence-breakery and cries of, "Move the damn dog earthward, Dickface!"

The metal plates on his back opened wide and I was tempted to lob in a grenade of warm hospitality and festive cheer. My thought being, "Why kill your evil neighbor when maybe he could just join the party?" But the clot in my right temporal lobe had been on blood-thinners for weeks, its running regimen having remained dirigible, and it chose that moment to break through. The doctors later said the blood flow destroyed parts of my ventral prefrontal cortex, removing any constraints I might have had for anger.

Ordwello thought he was pissed, but when I was through with him, he would be omicturated!

Only biting my tongue kept it from crawling out of Tooth Town, past the Vermillion Border, down my adrenaline-twitching torso, across the mixed fescue lawn, and up to Ordwello's throat. But using the Constrictor Feature I'd had newly installed in my mouth-meat would have ruined the show I'd planned for later, and I'd made too many bedeviled eggs to let that agenda collapse.

Instead I crouched to the ground, crab-scuttled back a stretch to the garden, and grabbed a spiked philosopher's stone. Then, noticing that Ordwello's back plates had now extended above him in a three story V, I shouted, "Adulterer!" and gave the barbed boulder a mighty huck.

I'd heard that, against the wishes of his doctors, he'd had second tots on the eve of his third skelephant removal. It was a good thing for me he hadn't gone through with it, I thought, watching my mighty thought-bender pass between his second and third plate of beans (Why he carried his food around on his back was anyone's guess). As the stone slipped between his vertebrae and passed into the spinal fluid he normally filled his lighter with, my friends cowered in the pool to avoid the blast of reason when it went off.

I was not so lucky. Ordwello had told me of his involuntary Gumball Punctures before—all of those extra holes meant that the spinal fluid would be improperly pressurized. The explosion would be as vast and luminescent as a deep sea fish that learned to breakdance.

And, lo, it was! An obviously female personal-sized purple mushroom clowd rose from his back. And I knew my only option was to tell her a clock-clock joke.

"How many clock-clocks does it take for a Zen Master to—"

"Woof!"

Shit! I was still holding his wriggly non-cooked pupkin, who had just startled the briefly mesmerized nuclear blast. And knocked over my iced tea! There would be hell to pay (or purgatory to rent, at a minimum) if I did not act fast.

These little nuclear crises do flair up from time to time and are usually not apocalyptic. I tried to reason with her. "Clearly, madam, I am an amalgam, much like what the dentist uses to fill your teeth." I was in a hurry and couldn't think of anything else to say, but she stopped expanding and I seemed to have her attention, so I continued. "To indicate otherwise would trigger other whys you don't want answered. With that said, may I suggest that our friend Ordwello is not worth getting all hot and bothered over. Certainly not while there's a nice pool in which to cool your heels and refreshments to be had."

The great cloud hesitated, and so, yes, I confess to raising public spirit at the point of a gun. With my non-pupkin-yielding, extra sticky paste-hand I reached for the flare gun tucked away in the cottony wasteland of my E.T. Eliot brand waistband.

One pull on the trigger unleashed a trolley of chugging Acquiescence Bullets.

"All aboard my positive suggestion!"

I flopped flat to the ground, semi-mindful of my fistful of pupkin as bullets knocked chunks out of the cloud's cheese-cake smile. Twelve purple swirling death's heads nodded in agreement.

"A swim does sound lovely," they multi-phonically remarked.

My guests never predicted nuclear boiling annihilation, otherwise they surely would have posed in more pretty-making fashions, chasing the ever-present ambition to be the most be-coming of the dead.

And so it was that the lobster-pot frenzy of hidden guest, chlorinated water, and pleasant atomic expansion met in a mil-lisecond of accidental malice and made mist of prior prob-lems.

With no one left to please, and no need to produce roast pupkin, Ordwello and I found ourselves death-quenched with little else to make of our evening. Noting the regrettable mess in my pool, I phoned the Queen's Service and employed sev-eral hirsute servants to fill the body bags.

After that, all was balmy evening and low-spoke words as we de-jawed the memories and made marionberry pies from our crumbling hearts.

"Woof!"

O, pupkin!

CONRAD'S NEW SHOE GOO

with Eric M. Witchey

For Conrad, Aunt Millicent's dark-tack candy house had become more hovel than home, a tiny compound overrun by militant vermin dedicated to her conspiracies of sex burning and the venal papoose. There, harmless humans, roasted and boiled to little cubes, offered sweet and ripe from altars strewn with tiny feet, graduated overboard into maudlin breast embraces.

His love for Aunt Millicent notwithstanding, thoroughbred doubt had tunneled into Conrad's washboard brain concerning the need to bribe the almighty infant with such benign souls. Once he'd been a true believer, but fervent prayers had become an iron gag and a drunkard of gin, rock bottom in an upended vermillion mine, giving solace to gnats of cherry absolution over his chalice of simian smoke. He drank it anyway—for spiritual spelunking was a hobbyhorse of last resort—then prepared for his wee, one-man exodus.

Tonight, while his aunt, escalators underneath, rallied the vermin faithful with the familiar broadside, raging at ice queens though she herself savored a frozen cocktail, he would trunk his pack and make good his mistake.

He bespectacled himself by stretching out his naked erection, all the while hankering after older and more popular atrocities. Thawing shrimp danced under tanning bed moonlight while netherwhales sang a serpentine dirge of liberty and blisterhood. Revolving doors, ever harvest to sunder, begin to end, with every apology a death penalty. Just once more, Conrad thought, as his glancing blows, outfitted for several expeditions to the summit, ran up and down his giant erection. At last glance, its Everest shadows glinted with the moment of sunrise in anticipation. Then, with the image of Aunt Millicent fixed in Conrad's mind, ticker-tape streamers and the resultant confetti pools of his release were a fitful and awkward parade of his quandary.

His heart could not remain so stretched between the territory of clown shoes and Poeish regrets. He hadn't screamed puppet warnings in over a decade, but, "Home," he decided loudly, "is where you wake unto waist rings and pyramid points, and where under cud-slathered ceilings dripping sweet clover yellow, a man can have four testicles instead of the usual tub of lard." Aunt Millicent's vermin hordes serenaded his enlightenment while unburdening his cast-iron trunk and feeding him a heresy of corndogs and a chocolate-dipped, high-end adultery appliance.

HER NAME

The woman's name could not be pronounced by any mouth but her own. Florence called her simply Wife, since that is what she was to him. By contract, they were bound to each other shortly after the birth of their first see-through daughter, and although he regretted his decision more each day, he expected their marriage to last forever. Lately, in the quiet hours of the night, Florence wept and picked nervously at the brittle entrance to his special escape hatch, that two mile disappearance zone which extended from his left elbow into the darkness to his right. The zone had been a gift from his great grandmother, and was to be used only if he could find no other solution to a problem. He could take advantage of it, but then what would they do with his dead body?

Florence had never had any feelings for Wife, and she had chosen him only because she collected runts of all animal types. Even so, he was ashamed of himself—after all, as one of their neighbors had pointed out to him, "Everyone like her here, likes her here."

True enough, but none of them had to live with her; they didn't have to wear special protective lenses just to look at her when her emotions flared, because she never gave her pyrotechnic displays on the street. They knew nothing of how she became when he didn't follow her specific household procedures—always hitting him with that stick and shouting, "Thems is the rules!" as she pointed to a sign she had tacked up in the den that read, THEMS IS THE RULES.

Conflict was sex for Wife; she argued for orgasm. And her roving eyes were everywhere, watching Florence, looking for a fight. One day, he discovered one in his pants pocket—and that was all she needed.

"Why must your rattle sneakers vomit on my housecoat?" she screamed. Without waiting for an answer, Wife cocked her jaw with a collapsible goat's meat sausage she stored in an enlarged pore in her forehead, then proceeded to shout the dirt right off the walls. To chase Florence from the house, she used her twelve tiny children as ammunition. Even their fragile see-through daughter was hurled at him. Chasing him down the street, she grabbed up those infants in good enough condition to use again and lobbed them once more.

As Florence slopped off like a gallon of milk worms, he heard her crying her little teeth out. "You'd better be home for dinner," she sobbed. "I've invited Hot Dog Vendor and Mr. Cheese!"

Totally dispirited, Florence went to the courthouse and purchased a street bum's license and the appropriate uniform. That night, he slept in an own-your-own dust and dismal dank stairwell downtown. But as he passed on into the small red and green sleep that vacationed between his eyes, he knew that his obscurity would be short-lived. The monstrous tangle of his slumber rose through the glassy evening as he dreamt fitfully of Wife. She was bent on dominating him, and her eyes would never cease to cast about until they had seen through his flimsy disguise and dragged him home again.

It was about mousenight when he awoke to a loud noise in his large intestine. He was sure it was a solution to his problem, and after crawling up out of his stairwell, he reeled out the length of his colon and considered the oracle. Then, deep in thought, watching yet not seeing the grey slippery things glide up and down, back and forth, across his tabletop city, Florence decided that the event he saw in his own waste should surely come to pass.

He looked around to see if there were any eyes watching. There was no humming or redness—as a matter of fact, nothing seemed usual—so Florence headed for home, creeping slowly across the table top, screaming from bone to bone.

The long, cylindrical light of day was just beginning to flicker in the sky when he got there. He entered the house quietly and caught Wife still asleep, inside the bed with Hot Dog Vendor and Mr. Cheese. To ensure her silence, he removed the goat's meat sausage from her forehead and fed it to his grandmother's sick starvation goat. Then, after dragging her from the bed, he wrapped her neatly in the oversized torso he'd been wearing since early childhood. "Folks will laugh at you, Flory," his mother had always said. "But one day that thing'll come in handy." And indeed it had.

Florence sold each of Wife's lovers a sizable portion of the other. As conjoined twins, they left, quite pleased with themselves and promising him silence out of both sides of their mouths.

The rest was easy—Florence carried Wife to the end of town and dropped her off the edge of the table. That would take care of her. No one had ever made it back from The Big Floor.

Time was time, and when after a horsey spell or two, the neighbors began to wonder aloud what had happened to Wife, Florence explained, "How do you think I got my toaster to work underwear?"

All the same, he led the townsfolk on a half-hearted search for Wife.

They spread out to the four corners of their world, each of them yelling, "Hey, you!"

"This effort was doomed from the start," the Mayor proclaimed moments later when the search was called off. "She could be lying dead in a ditch somewhere and she wouldn't even know it, because none of us can even pronounce her name."

Everyone went home and Wife was soon forgotten.

But Florence did not forget, and one morning, his underwear overworked and loose and his toaster exploding on the breakfast nook, Wife landed on his doorstep as if vaulted clear from the nether world.

Reluctantly, he let her in the door, and then listened to her voice.

"When you tossed me to The Big Floor," she said, "I fell to sick blazes and pitiful humor. For the longest time, I remained a puddle of flaming viscera. This gave me a chance to rechew all that I'd spat at you, a great puddle almost too deep to breathe. In doing so, I realized how impossible it was for others to pronounce my name."

"Yes," Florence agreed. "But I'd always thought that was just 'cause your face had a mind of its own."

"No, quite the opposite," she said. "I'd never been able to face myself until I saw my reflection in The Big Floor, and realized that because of my name, I'd always ripped myself apart from everyone. And so, I've decided to change my name."

"You could easily do that, but I'm almost certain I'll still recognize you, and so will everyone else."

"But at least my thin paper world will be wound onto a big white roll." She smiled her crude but effective smile. "What do you think of the name *Happy Face?*"

JUST A WET LAST NAME

It was the same morning I always awoke to and lately I was beginning to wonder if it was all worth it. There was the one option that everyone had and many took, but I didn't like to think about it.

I knew there would be people watching me from the window, so I awoke with a faked start, then darted for my underwear in an effort to conceal my true feeler. I chose the unwholesome between-meal slacks, a corrugated cardboard tunic and a seventeenth century brank. Within minutes I was dressed and ready for work.

Today was that holiday—I forget its name—when we observed the stars as one might the birthday of some patriot of local history. Folks should have been out celebrating the Crab Nebula or something, but instead they were loitering about my house, hoping to "get a glimpse." Why anyone would be so interested in what I did, I couldn't have told you, but it was like this every day. I caught a few peeking in as I picked my way down the hall toward the front door amidst the smell of pineapples rotting in tropical heat. What were they doing—or not doing—with all that fruit?

When I stepped outside, everyone pretended they hadn't been watching my every move since the moment I leapt out of bed. The old fart that masturbated on my front stoop asked if I wanted to trade Barbie Doll Barf-Alike Contest Trading Cards. I whipped out my deck and we went at it. Ultimately I got the better of the trade. Apparently satisfied, he zipped up his pants and moved on.

I swung around the pyre of a woman still smoldering in my front lawn and pressed myself into the throng of people filling the sidewalk and street beyond. I found my car and set out at a snail's pace so as not to run anyone down. The crowds stayed with me the whole way to work.

What I'd always liked about my job was that I wasn't popular. It was boring, but a nice contrast to what I found at home and on the streets. People at work ignored me, so I usually enjoyed a respite from all the attention.

When I got there, all the slots in the lot were taken and I had to park on the street where I carelessly lost an arm in a parking meter. And I knew if I didn't feed the meter periodically throughout the day I'd lose my car too. I wondered briefly what else I could afford to lose as I made my way inside the work place.

I forgot all about it when I discovered a damned office party going on. Worse, they weren't celebrating the Crab Nebula or any other celestial body. No, they were celebrating the death of my cubicle mate, Carter, in a freak copier accident. The machine had been giving us trouble for some time, doing little but folding, spindling, and mutilating employees. When they heard the characteristic sounds of its malfunction, the office manager, Jan, rushed to Carter's aid. Jan didn't reach him until he was giving off loud, National Anthem-type noises. By then it was too late.

I was terribly upset. Carter didn't like me, but he was my favorite person. Far from sympathetic, my boss, Fred, made me wear the green onion-scented underwear of shame and nothing else, just because I was late to work. He situated me in the center of the conference room with the party going on all around me.

I was pissed. I was saddened. But strangely that somehow made my day. This wasn't the same old day I always had.

The caterer stood in the corner, offering refleshments. He

oozed what he sold, then gushed up one mighty French fry. Six or Eight of my coworkers pounced and made short work of it.

Sylvia was rushing around making sure her dress would blow off in the slightest breeze.

Tedward, in a clot of giggling coworkers, took a joke about his pencil sharpener the wrong way and began to shed his skin angrily.

Someone was setting fire to peoples' clothing. The place filled with smoke and the alarms went off, producing a beat that combined awkwardly with the weak music coming through the sound system. Lenny and several others took advantage of this to contort about in a paroxysm of bad dance.

Sharp objects were being tossed around the room. It was Jessica trying to juggle various hand tools. I saw Lenny pocketing a butane lighter just as Jessica became distracted—her outfit was on fire—and she lost control. The implements went flying and Fred's eyes were put out by a sharp gardening tool and he went down. Jessica helped him to his feet, apologized, then hurried to the executive washroom to remove her burning outfit. Fred's wife, Sheryl, who had always wanted a blind husband, ran after Jessica to thank her. Jessica and Sheryl did not reappear for some time and when they did, there was obviously something going on between them.

As always, everyone was ignoring me, but having to maintain my seat in the middle of all this was gloriously nerve-wracking.

Finally when it all ended and the workday was done, my coworkers went home and, having forfeited my car, I was safely delivered to my house by magical means. It was the same night I always returned home to. I could feel them all watching me through the plumbing as I sat on the toilet that evening.

I considered the opt-out once again.

"Just a wet last name," I said aloud, then thought of everyone ignoring me at the office party and smiled. "Yes, life is just a wet last name, but that doesn't mean what it used to."

APPLEWIDE

When Applewide was first presented to me, I knew that no matter how astringent his caresses, how funny my fists, I would ultimately find his second floor entirely satisfactory and have to move in. But I resisted. Twice his eyes came for me and twice I made it known that Applewide's meantime was like no one else's. But friends wouldn't listen. Family wouldn't help. I reached for them, but though I could identify their limbs, I could not locate their shoulders.

With the ensuing years of my domestication, my elders wandered off and ghosts beat a retreat wherever I went. Applewide kept our cupboard full of unsung arguments and nightly took to wrestling with his armchair over a bloody stool.

Though his abuse exposed the wilted vegetables grown 'round my heart, I was curiously indifferent to the kind of nakedness he demanded.

My obligations to Applewide resulted in several cute but deadly toddlers. My remaining friends, all wearing an expression of delayed shock and blurting out a shiny "Please," timed out one by one. Each death took place while of one of my children hummed a suspicious lullaby.

Applewide and I festered together into unwrinkled pink, a pair of tiny black slippers drawn too tightly over too many feet. The toddlers never grew. They spit up their words without speaking them first. The sky buckled with the yaw and pitch of the world.

Then one night Anger pulled us over and Applewide was arrested for driving with a tumor. I'd never thought of myself that way before and was insulted. But the next day, oh happy day, on orders from Applewide's pre-trial physician, I was surgically removed.

HIS GRANDMOTHER'S EYES

"The one-eyed devil only sees in one direction," his grandma would say and point out the two eggs embedded in her face. Like her words, they were round sparkling ones that bounced around in their sockets. They were god-peeping and blood-bursting alive. He thought the best most people could do was paw at the dirt just inches from her face.

Along with the glossy orbs, Grandma sported six blue and purple sawmill tattoos, and her skink experiments had once saved the toenail industry. Back in the day, a mere glimpse of the bony plates of her wedding gown had caused 1920s megaphone crooners to swallow their own heads. Even when he was raised, she could still fire lap dogs from her armchair at blinding speeds. Spite for this was a waterproof woman who could not actually swim.

Now the boy was man and she had vacated the dumpling body and mind that could make him think sounds like an on and off willow switch. Living in an old age home, she was an abbreviated insect, a despondent gristle and bone twig waiting to die.

His love for his grandmother was a lumpy bindle-stiff that refused to chant. A misty death rumor, his growing hatred visited her every part. All but the baubles in her head. His club-footed johnny cakes still rose and fell whenever he saw them. He would beat her with whimsy sticks, but it would do no good.

One night he made it past the muggy wet nurse who was his grandmother's shadow. Grandma was stretching and yawning the dog saw and did not awaken even as he scratched away the socked grubs of her head.

He made out with his prize.

To cover his tracks, he fed them to himself, then went to pick them up.

A mistake, this led him to his pissed office box where he met his match and maker.

WHERE PINK IS FOR POODLES, APPLIANCE GENETICS APPLIES

with Kevin Ward

On the fifth morning, Swiveltop panicked. Before falling asleep, he had forgotten to draw an arrow in the dirt to indicate the direction he was traveling. The tunnel into which he had been magically transported stretched uninterrupted into the hazy distance in both directions. Even the woolly heath that grew on the walls showed no sign of his passage.

I have only the tail end of a coin's chance. If I choose the wrong direction, I have come this far for naught and will cease to have ever existed.

Frustration caused his head to spin. And then, with arms flung out to the sides, Swiveltop's torso began to spin while his feet and head remained stationary.

At one end of the tunnel lay his destination, Outhound. The other held only oblivion: The Will'ven't Bin.

Grabbing an ear in each of his metallic hands, he gave his head a wanton spin—where it pointed when it stopped, Swiveltop would go. It slowed and came to a stop facing the same direction as his feet. How convenient, he thought, beginning his silly water sprinkler-inspired gait. He quickly shifted into high gear and was making good time as he tried to put the fear of being lost out of his mind—he could not bear the thought that he might miss the gathering at Outhound, where dogs contained nothing.

Swiveltop had found himself in this lonely tunnel after

insulting his clan's proud snaggleman. The old goat had pronounced the sacred words improperly and Swiveltop had tried to straighten the soothsayer's toothprayer. Now, he had been given a choice: carry the clan's powerful Magic Marker to the gathering at Outhound, or seek oblivion.

He would know that he had chosen correctly when he saw one of the ancient signs that read OUTHOUND TRAFFIC KEEP LEFT, or EXIT RAMP DO NOT STOP.

Swiveltop leapt fences and stone walls, burrowed through ancient Indian mounds, bone chips and flint tools flying, until the tunnel was as wide as a small lamb's glottis (a fact he quickly gleaned from his lazy rotisserie ancestral memory).

He took heart as he didn't seem to recognize any of this territory.

When he came to a long downhill run, Swiveltop stored his legs in their special hide-a-limb compartments, fell on his side and started rolling, his backpack flapping like a fabled retread as he picked up speed.

But then he came upon the rusted, broken ruin of a streetlamp—one that he was sure he had seen in the tarry, pipe-stem grottoes of the previous day. Swiveltop cursed himself and the powerful, pink Magic Marker in his backpack for not reminding him to mark his way before his Big Rotary Sleep. His thoughts spun as his head and body were prone to do.

Okay, if I'm going the wrong way, that doesn't mean I have to go all the way to The Will'ven't Bin. If I retrace myself a little to get my bearings, won't that just make me seem more substantial?

As he stood, wondering if indecisiveness were death, he heard a spattering sound ahead. Curiosity consumed him and, forgetting himself, he moved forward on his pontoon pile sea legs through a lumpy, sweating dough pond. Peering to either side into the darkness, he moved slowly through the brown, toxic dough.

Rounding a corner, he found the source of the spattering—a long, thin, horse-headed whistle with umbrella wings, stepladder legs, and jellyfish eyes. The being shut its wings, curbing the drops of pungent rain flowing from its underside. With a ring, it casually flicked a clinging glob of uncooked rye from one of its lower rungs. A deep note sounded and echoed throughout the chamber.

It then removed the mummified thumb of a primate from a chain around its thin, chromium neck and, with an exaggerated show of ceremony, pointed it in the direction Swiveltop was moving. Looking expectant, the whistle-being said, "Hoot!"

Something within Swiveltop told him that hoot was the sound made by an extinct animal reputed to be very wise. Naturally, he assumed that this was such a beast, that it might understand his problem and offer a solution. He stopped and allowed the whistle-being to climb aboard.

Its ladder legs were poorly designed for climbing and the hooter used its mouth to get a better grip. Sharp, horsey canines cut into the backpack strap. Already frayed and unraveled from long, rough days of rolling, the pack fell, carrying with it the precious Magic Marker, and sank slowly into the swiftly rising dough.

Before Swiveltop could bend and grab for it, a small herd of snowshoe-shod tripods, sporting TV antennae draped with tinsel and Christmas lights, stampeded by, trampling the dough and obscuring the depression made by the sinking backpack.

As he frantically swam through the now-soupy dough, searching the tunnel floor for the precious article, the hooter merely sat astride him, whistling the theme of an old cowboy show that was just being received by fog-hoppers and leaf-ladders in the Lesser Magellanic Cloud.

Swiveltop's middle hand wrapped around an object in the dough and the hooter on his back said, "Hee!" He thought this to be some sort of signal and yanked the object out of the dough with a squish. Relieved, he joyfully spun around and around, whipping the dough into a disgusting pinkish-brown gluten.

"Humph?" Swiveltop said when he had slowed down enough to get a good look at the strapless bra he had come up with. After a moment's thought, he offered it to the hoooter.

"Humph, humph, humph," it hummed, mocking Swiveltop as its eyes explored the dough-smeared satin lace and cleavage bow.

Swiveltop, dumbfounded, forgot his search as he watched the hooter clean the bra and roll it into a rod of dough-piercing light with which it began to pick its teeth. Several hours passed before it dawned on Swiveltop that he could use this light to search for the Magic Marker.

He reached up to take it from his passenger, but the hooter held on, uttering a confused "Honk!"

In the inevitable fumble, the light fell from their grasp. Where it landed, the dough was pierced to the heart. It let out a moist burp of pain and withdrew down the tunnel, leaving a trail of wet, pink flour.

Outraged, Swiveltop spun after it, nearly dislodging the hooter in his haste. Dangerously, the whistle being swung upside-down by its teeth from Swiveltop's radiator grill.

The pursuit took them through heathy hells and then a forest of rolled-up red and green windsocks which flapped wildly and snapped painfully on their bare behinds. The dough, ever elusive, climbed stairs through organs that Swiveltop could not even name.

As the dough moved in its kneading gallop, it became pinker and pinker and Swiveltop realized that the Magic Marker had lost its top and was leaking. He redoubled his efforts, the wind of his passage hooing through his rider's slightly parted lips.

The brilliant pink glob of dough, worn down and greatly diminished in size, came into view beyond a copse of stiff-standing sweat socks. It had stopped and was quivering and spitting out shreds of backpack material. Unable to break in time, Swiveltop grabbed the end of the backpack strap and was jerked to a sudden halt.

The hooter flew on, leaving its teeth behind. It screamed a desperate, "Hooah, hooah!" as it disappeared through an arch down the tunnel.

Swiveltop pulled hard on the strap and the dough came to him like an empty dog on a leash. The dough-ball had been worn down, exhausted. All that remained now was to carve it into usable portions and then excavate the Magic Marker. He knew that the hunks of dough would help feed the empty dogs at the gathering. After repairing the strap with a bit of bindersniff adhesive, he loaded the dough into what remained of the backpack.

Cleaning the gummy, pink gluten from his delicate hands, he found the Magic Marker under the nail of his left pinky. The powerful writing implement had obviously been drawn there by the colorful name of the digit.

Its top was missing and it was out of ink and Swiveltop knew that he had failed the snaggleman and his entire clan. He flung the Magic Marker from him in despair and waddled slowly down the tunnel, seeking oblivion within The Will'ven't Bin.

And oblivious he was as he entered a broader area with brighter light and the urgent sound of yapping. The walls changed from industrial heath to brick and chain-link fence. He paused in a chamber filled with dog-ear documents and slide samples from of ancient hydrants. Orange light filtered through hair-festooned windows.

Absently, as he thought of what must inevitably come, he passed from this chamber into a great vault heaped with mounds of bone, sinew, and viscera. Negotiating a moist course through this area, he exited through a dilating aperture, rolling and twisting as if surfing peristaltic waves.

He came out into bright light that beat down on him as did the barking of furry, many-limbed, empty leather pillow cases. Swiveltop surrendered himself sadly to what he now recognized to be empty dogs. He tossed the backpack to them so they could see that he had lost the Magic Marker and could no longer fill them in.

The empty dogs flopped forward, a pack of bags wrestling for the baggy pack and its contents. The first to find the pink dough gulped it down ravenously and immediately began to stiffen and swell. One by one, each dog had a turn with the dough until all were full.

At that moment, it came to Swiveltop, with all the knowledge he would need for his new station in life, that this was what the senile, old snaggleman had planned all along.

He took the teeth the hooter had thoughtfully left in his grill, jammed one tooth between each of his own and then stood amidst the gathering of expectant dogs. Now he could pronounce the sacred words.

"Fetch, Boy," he shouted.

FRANKLY

Kevin A. Ward

Frankly couldn't have been more lonely had he attended the Eternal Hood Ornament Factory Dance legless. He partook only of himself, not wanting anyone to know he expelled waste, while shame ate him inside-out and left him with a lisping personality and no friends.

One day, during a particularly solitary summer lunch, a star named Barney appeared in the heavens and Frankly was inspired to toss his meal ticket into the sky. With that, the wicked young girl-head, Webby, appeared before him.

"Dear gentle man," she said, "My charming end fully holds our boastful ecstasy. Would you Parfait with me?"

Frankly had never been good at digesting himself while such a vision swam before his eyes. Her ceaseless banter and obvious manner replaced his with cold feet and mammal hands. This girl-head wanted him, but with that pending, he was silenced like the periodic blatting of a cagey zither. He blushed moistly pink as he conspicuously admired her blousy brush fire pantaloon constrictors which so buoyantly offset her quaking membrane. As she made small talk, his tightly concealed vapor head sprouted violently and he shook in hangnail angst.

With fish-scaled hedge bait she led him to farm fronds and tender comfort cloth in the road, where he pretended full knowledge of the broad, meaty kind. Webby seemed totally unaware of his green-giggle ineptitude, leading him to make jokes worth millions. Soon their four humors swam together in the street.

Finally spent and destitute, they lay in the open, sodden street, like the black spindly cinders of burnt spiders. Frankly, believing he was in love, screamed out all of his previous lonely meals. Webby gulped them down, then got up to leave.

"No," Frankly said. "You must stick to me." But Webby withdrew her tacky silk and turned away.

The white fluff that billowed from Frankly's swollen heart powdered the street like the dander of animals meant to melt in the mouth. That she might have no more for him was far more than he'd ever felt capable of wishing he were up to living through . . . or so he thought before their combined humor leapt up from the road to frighten him.

This squish monster, an ancient evil foretold by graffiti sticks the world over, climbed to Webby's breastly cheeks, mouthing a threat to all humankind with its swift suckling size. Within moments the creature had yawned out its first tooth and it locked onto her nippled dewlaps. By the time thunderous coffee cracks and breakfast jokes heralded its second tooth, the brute was large enough to devour the girl-head and did so in one bite. Within mere days it would be large enough to stomp the town and kill the one million who burned their brains within it.

It's kill or be killed, Frankly told himself. And so the long deadly scar that ran through his bloodline emerged and Frankly began his killing spree as the Barney star rose higher. He would kill a million people.

What became of this man-slick and his prodigious progeny after that? Was he a hero for saving all others from death at the hands of the squish monster, his deeds to be celebrated every time Barney appeared in the heavens? We will never know, for his spree claimed the hairy host of holy folk who determined such things, and no one else survived to express an opinion.

ABOUT THE AUTHOR

Alan M. Clark was born in Nashville, Tennessee in 1957. He grew up in a home full of old bones, Indian relics, and dusty medical books.

In 1984 he became a freelance illustrator, and has since produced artwork ranging in subject from fantasy, science fiction, horror, and mystery for publishers of fiction, to cellular and molecular biology for college textbooks.

A winner of the World Fantasy Award and four Chesley Awards, Clark has illustrated the writing of such authors as Ray Bradbury, Robert Bloch, Joe R. Lansdale, Stephen King, George Orwell, Manly Wade Wellman, Greg Bear, Edward Lee, Peter Straub, and Lewis Shiner.

His short fiction has appeared in anthologies such as *Last Drink Bird Head, The Thackery T. Lambshead Pocket Guide to Eccentric and Discredited Diseases, Portents, Bedtime Stories to Darken Your Dreams, More Phobias, The Book of Dead Things, Dead on Demand,* and *Darkside,* and also to the magazines *Midnight Hour* and *The Silver Web.*

Currently, he and his wife Melody reside in Eugene, Oregon.

Visit him online at www.alanmclark.com.

LaVergne, TN USA
10 March 2011
219558LV00002B/46/P